Sitting in Professor Orinaca's small dark office, Hank felt uneasy. The old dusty books on the tall shelves seemed to lean in on him. The skull on the professor's desk looked very much like a human one.

The professor reached out, and Hank handed him the package. As Orinaca began untying the string around it, Hank couldn't help noticing how the man's hands trembled. *What could be inside the box to make him so excited?* wondered Hank.

Hank watched Orinaca unwrap the brown paper. He took off the lid of a cardboard box and lifted out something wrapped in newspaper. The professor's eyes narrowed as he unwrapped the package. Then they opened wide as Orinaca held up an object that wasn't like anything Hank had ever seen.

cover illustration by
Richard Kriegler

Published by Worthington Press
7099 Huntley Road, Worthington, Ohio 43085



Printed in the United States of America
10 9 8 7 6 5 4 3 2

ISBN 0-87406-391-4

# Contents

## CHAPTER 1

# *The Pearl-Handled Knife*

HANK COOPER didn't like the man's looks. A big, stocky man the size of a linebacker, he was wearing a grease-stained, black suit. His thick, dark beard and mustache couldn't hide the scar that ran across his suntanned face from his flat nose to his torn left ear. The man was leaning against a pillar. He had one hand in his pants pocket. In the other hand he held a long, thin pearl-handled knife. He was using it to clean his ugly, yellowed teeth.

Hank found himself staring for a moment at the man. Even worse, the man was staring at him. Hank shivered as their eyes met.

Hank was 12 years old, almost 13, and tall for his age. His black hair hung down from under his Chicago Bears cap. Hank wore khaki cargo pants, a green T-shirt, and carried a backpack. After a moment, he tore his eyes away from the man and watched his mother walk to a wall of lockers. Stealing another glance at Scarface, he noticed the man was watching her, too.

Hank saw his mother take a key out of her purse and open one of the lockers. Reaching inside, she lifted out a box. It was about the size of a shoebox, wrapped in brown paper and tied with string. After studying the unopened box for a moment, his mother carried it to him.

"Hank, look after this for a few minutes," she told him. "But don't open it. Our plane leaves pretty soon, and I have to go to the restroom. Don't forget what I told you to do if we get separated."

Hank remembered what his mother had told him. *But why would they get separated?* he wondered.

Hank held the package in his lap as he sat on a bench and waited for his mother to return. This was his first trip out of the United States. His parents, Jeff and Julie Cooper, were archaeologists at the Institute of Antiquities in Chicago. Their expeditions to study ancient civilizations took them all over the world. Hank had always wished that they would take him along on one of their treasure-hunting trips. Now here he was. But this trip wasn't like any other treasure hunt. What they were looking for was his father. He had disappeared somewhere in the jungles of Bolivia.

Hank's mother hadn't been able to tell him very much about his father's disappearance. She received a telegram from their friend in Bolivia, Professor Carlos Orinaca. He reported only that Hank's dad had failed to reach a village in the jungles of Bolivia on an expedition. He was presumed lost or even dead.

Hank's mother decided to fly down to help search for her husband. Professor Orinaca tried to talk her out of it, saying the jungles were too dangerous for her to be in without her husband, but Hank's mother insisted on going. Figuring she could use Hank's help, she decided to take him along.

Hank's mother let him in on a secret before they left Chicago. Before he had left on the expedition, Hank's dad had told his wife that if anything happened to him, she was to go to Bogota, Colombia, and claim the contents of a locker in the airport terminal. He left her a key for the locker, and he said that she was not to tell anyone about it.

Now Hank held that package in his hands.

Turning the box over in his hands, Hank

wondered what was in it. He hated to think of his father being lost in the wild jungles of Bolivia. He had read about the jaguars and pumas, the alligators, and the snakes like the boa constrictor and giant anaconda that were large enough to easily crush a person.

He looked up to see the man with the scar staring at him again. Was it only his imagination, or was the man staring at the package in his lap? He felt a cold sweat come over him, and he tightened his grip on the package.

He watched Scarface light up a thin, brown cigar and begin puffing on it. Scarface never took his eyes off the package that Hank held. Then the man began opening and shutting the pearl-handled knife. Coolly, the man looked away from Hank and knocked the ash off his cigar.

To take his mind off the ugly man staring at him, Hank looked around the terminal. Foreign airports were busy places with planes from many countries arriving and departing. And they were full of strange people from strange places. He saw a short, brown Indian with a colorful blanket thrown over his shoulder. A policeman or army officer with a shiny, leather shoulder holster walked past him. A short, fat lady in a peasant dress was holding a crying baby in her arms.

"Attention all passengers. Flight 918 to Lima, Peru, and La Paz, Bolivia, is now ready for boarding at gate 11."

Hank was glad to hear that. Finally, their plane was ready to board. He'd get away from this weird man. Hank looked at his watch. His mother had already been gone almost five minutes. He held the package tighter and hoped she would turn up soon.

After a few more minutes, Hank tucked the package under his arm and began walking toward the women's restroom.

He figured that his mother had heard the announcement to board. Airport restrooms always have loudspeakers in them. *But why wasn't she coming out?*

Hank approached the women's restroom. But suddenly he felt someone bang into him from behind. The impact spun him around.

A big lady in a floral-patterned dress the size of a three-man tent hovered over him, apologizing in what he thought was German.

"I'm in a hurry," the huge woman said in broken English. Brushing past him, she charged on toward the women's restroom.

"So am I!" Hank called after her. "My mom's inside. Would you tell her we're gonna miss our plane unless she hurries?"

"Ja, I'll tell her," the woman said gruffly and entered the washroom.

Hank paced back and forth outside the restroom door. After another few minutes, he heard the voice on the loudspeaker repeat the boarding call for Peru and Bolivia.

Finally, after what seemed to be hours, the German lady emerged from the restroom.

"What did she say?" Hank asked.

Ignoring him, the woman gave Hank a blank look and brushed by him.

"Hey! My mother!" Hank called after her loudly. "Is she coming out? We're gonna miss our plane!"

Impatiently, over her shoulder, the woman called back and shook a finger at him. "Bad boy! That wasn't nice to play a game on me. There wasn't anyone in there."

*That woman has to be lying,* Hank thought. *Mom's got to be in there!*

He opened the door slowly and walked in, calling out for his mother. He circled the room, looking for any sign of her. But the German woman was right. The room was empty!

*Mom must have gone out,* he thought. *While I was looking after the fat lady. She must not have seen me.*

He started to leave the washroom, and then

he saw something on the floor under a sink. He picked up a small, round case. He recognized it from the daisies painted on it. It was his mother's powder puff case. He stuffed it in his pocket and hurried out of the restroom. Outside, he walked in circles, looking for his mother. But he didn't see her anywhere in the terminal.

A sinking feeling suddenly swept over Hank. He was all alone in a foreign airport, and his plane was taking off in just a few minutes. What was he going to do? Should he find that man who looked like a police officer and tell him that his mother had disappeared? If he did that, he'd miss the plane.

Then he remembered what his mother told him earlier...

*If for any reason we get separated...if somehow I don't make it back to the plane...you board, Hank. Take the box to La Paz, to Professor Orinaca at the University of Bolivia. You can trust him. But don't trust anyone else. I'll meet you there...*

Hank told himself that somehow he and his mother had just lost track of each other in the crowded terminal. She must be looking for him, just as he was looking for her.

He had his ticket. He had the box. He

had his instructions. He knew what to do.

His heart pounding, holding the box firmly under an arm, Hank ran through the terminal, searching for the correct departure gate. He was sure that his mother would be there, waiting for him.

Hurrying through a crowd of people, Hank felt someone push hard against his back. He stumbled forward. The box flew out from under his arm. As he struggled to regain his balance, he watched as the box went sailing across the slick terminal floor. Then he saw an athletic young man in a white suit make a dive for the box.

Hank threw himself forward with both hands outstretched. The man in white was quick, but Hank was quicker. Hank grabbed the box just in time.

For an instant, the man in white looked at him. Hank got a good look at the man. He had blond hair and a thin, blond mustache. He looked very different from the short, dark South Americans.

Then the young man turned around and fled into the crowd of people that was passing by.

Hank looked after him for a moment, wondering why so many people were so interested in his package and what was inside it.

Then, holding the box tightly under his arm again, he hurried on, knowing he only had moments to get to gate 11.

Out of breath, he reached the departure gate and looked at a line of people passing through it to board the jet. But he didn't see his mother anywhere.

A boarding attendant was about to close the gate when he hurried through it. Hank gave the man his ticket, held the box snugly under his arm, and followed behind the last of the other passengers.

"Can you hold the plane until my mother gets here?" he asked a flight attendant.

"I'm sorry, but we have to keep to our schedule," the woman replied.

Hank walked quickly up and down the aisle in the plane, but he didn't see his mother. Now he knew he was stuck. He had to stay on the plane even without her. Hank took an aisle seat near the rear. Buckling up his seat belt, he looked out and glued his eyes on gate 11 in the terminal. There was still no sign of his mother.

Looking across the aisle, Hank caught his breath when he saw someone he did recognize. Scarface was sitting in the aisle seat across from him. When their eyes met, the man gave Hank a mean look.

A moment later, Hank heard a familiar voice behind him. "Bad boy," a woman said in a thick German accent.

The large woman from the restroom was taking up the aisle seat behind him, and then some.

"Playing games," she said, frowning at him.

The flight attendant was giving instructions about emergency procedures when Hank saw a passenger walking toward the aisle seat right in front of him. It was the young man in the white suit.

As the plane began taxiing along the runway, the sinking feeling swept over Hank again. He was all alone in a strange world, with no one to help him. His mother was gone. Hank shivered. He had a vision of his father, hacking his way through a Bolivian jungle with a machete, being stalked by a jaguar, and then being crushed by a monstrous anaconda.

All Hank knew for sure was that he was all alone now, on a jet, climbing into the blue sky over South America. He was surrounded by three strange people who seemed to have more than a passing interest in him. When Hank saw the three exchange glances, he began to get the feeling that it was definitely no coincidence that they were on the same plane that he was.

## CHAPTER 2
# *Skulls and Photographs*

WHEN the clouds parted and he could see the land below, Hank looked down, hoping to see mysterious markings on the ground. He had read that there were strange, unexplained drawings of birds or snakes carved in the ground in Peru and other countries. But he didn't see any markings. All he saw was Scarface's reflection in the window.

After a brief stop in Lima, Peru, Hank's plane landed at the airport in La Paz. He gripped his package tightly and tried to lose himself in a crowd of passengers who were getting off the airplane. When he had reached the long hallway leading to the terminal, Hank felt an arm under his, leading him forcefully through a terminal gate. He saw that the man in the white suit was pushing him along through the hallway. Right behind him were

Scarface and the fat German lady.

"Don't give us any trouble, kid!" the blond man warned Hank.

Hank felt the package being taken from under his arm. Desperately, he reached into his pants pocket and took out his mother's powder puff case. Opening it, he blew the powder in the face of the man in the white suit. The man cried out and began sneezing. He let go of the package and Hank's arm.

Hank grabbed the package and made a run for it into the large crowd of passengers in the terminal. Outside, Hank hailed a taxi. Moments later, the driver was taking him to the University of Bolivia. He kept looking out the rear window, but he didn't see any car following them. He sat back in his seat and let out a sigh while clutching the package.

At the university, Hank asked directions of some passing students who spoke English. He found his way to the office of Professor Carlos Orinaca in the Archaeology department. Hank knocked on a door at the end of a long, dark hallway.

The door was opened by a tall, thin, friendly-looking man with a deep tan and thick, black hair and a thin mustache. He looked surprised when Hank told him who he was.

"Come in," the professor said. "I'm very glad to meet you. Your father is one of my oldest friends. But where is your mother?" he asked.

Hank explained about everything that happened at the airport, happy to find someone who was a friend. Hank asked if his mother had gotten in touch with the professor.

"No," Orinaca said, offering Hank a seat next to his desk. "I've had no word from her."

The day was hot and steamy, and the small office was not air-conditioned. Hank felt like he was in a steam bath.

Hank looked around the small, cluttered office. There were shelves all the way to the ceiling, filled with dusty old books. On the desk and on top of some cases lay old bones and even a couple of skulls. Some looked like skulls of animals, but Hank thought the one on the professor's desk was a human skull.

Framed photographs of expeditions hung on the walls. On the professor's desk, Hank saw a photo of his father and mother with Orinaca at the base of what he supposed was some jungle temple.

"That was taken two years ago," Orinaca told him. "On an expedition to Cuzco, once an Inca capital."

Hank remembered when his parents went

on that trip. He had wanted badly to go with them, but they said the jungles were too full of wild animals and other dangers to take him along.

"How about my father?" Hank asked anxiously. "Have they found him yet?"

Orinaca shook his head. "I'm afraid not. And I'm sorry to say that the authorities have called off the search for him. Your father was lost near where this picture was taken, in very remote, dense jungle. Not even many natives live there."

Hank was almost afraid to hear the professor's answer, but he asked, "Have you given up hope of finding him, too?"

Professor Orinaca looked sympathetic. "I didn't mean that. And I haven't given up hope. Your father is a very clever man. If anyone could find his way out of the jungles of the interior, it would be your father."

"But there's no search party out looking for him now?" Hank asked.

Orinaca frowned. "I'm afraid the authorities have called off the rescue mission. They've been searching for nearly a week. I got back last night from the mountains where the search was stopped. Your father and I have been friends for many years," Orinaca continued sadly. "You must believe that I've done all I can to find him. I'm afraid there's nothing more anyone can do. But I haven't given up hope that your father will find his way out. And neither should you."

It wasn't much, but the professor's words made Hank feel a little bit hopeful.

"I'm sure your mother will call here any time now," Orinaca assured Hank. "I wouldn't worry about her. South American airports can be hectic places. This isn't the first time travelers have been accidentally separated."

The professor then pointed at the package that Hank was still holding. "I see you've brought the package," he said.

"Oh, you know about it?" Hank asked. "I thought it was supposed to be a secret."

"Your father told me about it, before he left for the jungle. Shall we open it?"

"Don't you think we should wait until my mom is here?" Hank asked.

"Oh, no, I think it's important we open it," Orinaca replied. "It may give us a clue about where your father is."

*That was different*, Hank thought. He couldn't imagine how what was in the package could help them find his father. But he was ready to try anything that might help. And besides, his mother had told him that he could trust the professor.

Orinaca reached out, and Hank handed him the package. As the professor began untying the string around it, Hank couldn't help noticing how the man's hands trembled.

*What could be inside the box to make him so excited?* Hank wondered.

He watched Orinaca unwrap the brown paper. He took off the lid of a cardboard box and lifted out something wrapped in newspaper. The professor's eyes narrowed as he unwrapped the paper, and they opened wide as he held up an object that wasn't like anything Hank had ever seen.

"The Dagger of Death!" Orinaca exclaimed.

Hank looked closely at the object. It was a carved gold and ivory handle. A large red gemstone in the handle caught the sunlight from a window and looked almost on fire. The professor cradled the dagger carefully in the palm of his hand.

"It's over a thousand years old," Orinaca explained in a low voice. "The high priest of the Zi Xen tribe used it to make sacrifices to their Sun God."

"Who made these sacrifices?" Hank asked.

"The Zi Xen were a tribe in Bolivia who lived even before the Incas. They lived in the highest, most remote part of the country in the Andes mountains near Lake Titicaca," explained the professor. "The Zi Xen lived in the jungles near Tiahuanaco, which later became the capital of a part of the Inca empire. Your father was on an expedition to Isla del Sol when he vanished."

"Isla del Sol?" Hank asked.

"It means Island of the Sun," the professor translated. "It's the largest island in Lake Titicaca. Isla del Sol is believed to have been the home of the Zi Xen. Later the island became the cradle of the Inca civilization. Some survivors of the Zi Xen civilization may still live on Isla del Sol."

Hank tried to follow everything that the professor was saying.

"Your father made several trips to Bolivia to search for the Zi Xen," Orinaca said. "He hoped to find some trace of their temples or villages and, perhaps, their incredible dagger."

"And the Zi Xen worshipped the sun as a god," Hank confirmed. "They sacrificed to the Sun God by killing animals with this Dagger of Death," Hank added.

"They didn't sacrifice only animals, Hank," Orinaca warned.

"You mean that this knife has killed people, too?" Hank asked in a whisper. A shiver ran up his spine, even though it was so hot in the professor's office that he could barely breathe. "Then this dagger must be very valuable," Hank said.

The professor nodded and began to look more closely at the carving on the dagger's gold and ivory handle. Then Orinaca picked up a magnifying glass from his desk and studied the handle more carefully.

"The Dagger of Death has been valued at three million American dollars. People have been looking for it for centuries. Men have killed for it," said the professor, looking up from the magnifying glass. "And your father was looking for it when he disappeared."

Hank saw the professor begin to frown, as he returned to studying the handle through the magnifying glass.

"Yes, Hank," said the professor with a strange look on his face. "The Dagger of Death is almost priceless."

Then he lowered the magnifying glass and said, "This dagger, however, is worth about $20."

CHAPTER 3

# *A New Friend*

"WHAT!?!" shouted Hank.

"This dagger is a fake," Professor Orinaca answered.

"But why would Dad leave us a fake dagger?" he asked. "What's going on? Is he in danger because of this fake dagger? You've got to help me find him, Professor Orinaca!"

The professor didn't answer. He studied the dagger some more through his magnifying glass.

"There's no question about it, unfortunately," he replied after taking another long look at the dagger. "It's not the original. It's only a copy."

"How can you tell?" Hank asked.

Orinaca showed him the handle. "Look here. The ruby isn't real. It's just glass."

It looked real enough to Hank. The red stone was set in the heart of a large bird of prey with its wings outstretched that was carved into the ivory handle of the dagger.

"The bird isn't right, either," the professor said. Hank gazed at the beautiful small figures that were carved into the ivory. "What's not right about the bird?" he asked.

"The boa constrictor in the left claw and the monkey in the right claw are authentic," Orinaca allowed. "But the bird isn't. On the handle of this dagger, it's an eagle. On the real Dagger of Death, there's a condor."

"How can you tell the difference?" Hank asked.

Professor Orinaca took a book down from a shelf and showed Hank two photographs. "The eagle is on the left, and the condor is on the right. You can see that the condor is much bigger. But the biggest difference is, unlike the eagle, the condor has black feathers, with white wing and neck markings."

The professor shook his head while Hank looked at the carving of the bird under the magnifying glass. "You might as well keep this fake dagger for a souvenir," Orinaca said. "I doubt it's even worth $20."

"But where did the fake dagger come from, Professor? Who made it, and why?" Hank asked.

"I don't know," the professor answered

quickly. "I wish I knew."

Then Hank said, "Some people at the airport in Bogota must have thought it was worth more than $20. They tried to steal it from me."

"What do you mean?" Orinaca asked, looking surprised.

"They were two men and a woman. They tried to take the box away from me in the terminal while I was looking for my mother," answered Hank.

Orinaca thought for a moment. "They couldn't have known what was in the box. They probably just thought it might be something valuable, something they could sell. Lots of pickpockets and thieves hang around airports down here," he explained.

"I don't know about that, Professor," said Hank. I have a feeling they knew what was in it. But they might have thought the dagger was the real thing, worth a fortune."

"Come now, Hank, how could strangers know what was in the box?" Orinaca asked. "And what makes you think they were working together? Maybe it's just your imagination."

"Well, it's something about the way they kept looking at each other in the airport and on the plane," Hank replied.

"Luckily, you escaped them and brought the box here to me," Orinaca said. "It's my guess they were just looking for anything they could steal. You'll never see them again."

Hank watched as the professor put the magnifying glass back in a drawer. "Of course, I'll help you find your father," Orinaca assured him. "I haven't given up hope of finding him. He may even turn up on his own." The professor got up and went around to the other side of his desk. He put a comforting arm around Hank's shoulder. "Your mother, too," he said.

Hank felt a little better, trusting that his father's friend would help him. But he wondered, *How can the professor be so sure I'll never see those three people again?*

"I'm pretty tired. I guess I'll go to the hotel. We have reservations at the El Dorado," Hank said, standing up. "I'll just wait there, until my mom comes or calls."

"Won't you stay at my home instead?" Orinaca asked with a smile. "I feel responsible for you, until your mother arrives."

Hank said he'd rather stay at the hotel, so his mother would know where to find him. He also wondered if the professor's house was as small and dusty as his office was.

"Here are my home and office phone

numbers," Orinaca said, jotting them down. "Call whenever you wish. And let me know the minute you hear from your mother. We'll have dinner together. I'll call you at your hotel."

Hank shook hands with Professor Orinaca and said good-bye.

"There's one more thing, Hank," the professor said. "Don't worry. We'll find your parents."

Hank left the university and took another taxi to the El Dorado, which was not far away in the center of the city. He could tell from just the short ride that La Paz was a large and busy city. Most of the people looked poor.

Checking in at the hotel, Hank asked the desk clerk if there was any message for him. But the clerk said that there was none. Hank rode an elevator up to the 12th floor. Unlocking the door to the suite of rooms, Hank looked around. He was glad the rooms were air-conditioned.

He threw his backpack on the bed and walked over to the balcony. Standing 12 stories above the roar of traffic, Hank looked down at the tiny people. He looked out over the city as far as he could see. Mountains rose in the distance. Standing alone on the balcony, he began to feel very alone again and wondered when he would be with his mother and father again. *They had to be safe*, he told himself. *They would come to the hotel soon. They just had to!*

By now it was midafternoon, and one thing began to crowd the feeling of loneliness out of Hank's mind. He was hungry. It had been hours and hours since he had last eaten. Not wanting to leave his room in case his mother called, Hank phoned room service and ordered a double cheeseburger, fries, and a soda pop to be delivered to his rooms.

While waiting for his food, he turned on the television set but found mostly Spanish-language soap operas. He found one station showing an American cowboy movie, but all the actors were speaking Spanish. Hank watched it for a while, but soon he found that one of the villains looked like Scarface from the airport. He switched off the TV and turned on the radio. He searched the dial for some American rock music. But all he could tune in were trumpets playing what sounded like bullfight music.

Finally, Hank heard a knock on the door. Opening the door, he was surprised to see a dark-skinned boy about his size. He was holding a tray with Hank's lunch. The boy was smiling broadly, showing a gap between two of his front teeth. His jet black hair hung down almost over his eyes from a wide forehead.

"You hungry, no?" the boy asked, handing Hank the tray. "I'm Pedro. You want nothing, you ask for me. I speak pretty bad English, you think?" Pedro laughed. "You Americans say something is *bad* when you mean *good*, no?"

It took Hank a moment to understand, and then he smiled. He knew what Pedro meant.

"Yeah, you speak English pretty *bad*."

Pedro looked Hank over and smiled again. "You must be rich, to come to my country and stay in a big hotel."

Hank laughed. "Hey, I'm not rich. I cut lawns or shovel snow back home in Chicago for my money. I wish I had a job like yours, where you get good tips."

"Not so good tips," Pedro said sadly. "But it's okay. If you're not rich, you no have to tip me. I be your *amigo* anyway."

Hank set the lunch tray down on a table and shook hands with Pedro.

"Okay, then," Hank said, "we're amigos. Hey, listen, why don't you stay? I could call for another order, and we could have lunch together."

Pedro hesitated at the door. "The same as

you?" he asked hopefully.

Hank laughed again, and then he phoned for another order. "But won't they expect you to pick it up?" he asked.

"I will," Pedro replied. "Then I stay and eat with you. Pretty 'bad,' man, huh?"

Within 15 minutes, Pedro had gone and was back again. And this time he had a lunch for himself. They sat on the balcony and talked while they ate. Pedro told Hank about his family and home. Hank learned that for generations Pedro's family had been what his people call *campesinos,* or peasants. Most of the Bolivians were either farming peasants or *mineros,* who worked the silver mines.

Pedro's father had been killed in one of the political revolutions, and he lived in a shack in the city with his mother and six sisters. He was the only one with a steady job. The others begged in the streets. Pedro liked working at the hotel because he could get good tips sometimes. He had also gotten a chance to learn some English.

Then Hank told Pedro about his own father and mother and how they had both disappeared. He told him about the expedition to find the Zi Xen and their sacrificial dagger.

"Jungle a bad place to be lost in," Pedro

said, frowning. Then his face brightened. "But your father find his way out. Or *we* find him."

"I don't know, Pedro," Hank said. "We're just kids. How could we find him?"

"I not go to school much," Pedro admitted. "But I know about Zi Xen. They live long ago. Some still live, they say. Deep in jungle far from here. But their Dagger of Death...that just legend. Like a, how you say, fairy tale. No *real* Dagger of Death!"

"My father was searching for it when he dropped out of sight," Hank explained. "Wait. I'll show you!"

He left his new friend on the balcony and went to his bedroom. Returning, he showed Pedro the fake dagger.

Pedro's black eyes grew wide at the sight of the gold and ivory dagger with the bright red gemstone shining in the handle.

"The Dagger of Death!" Pedro exclaimed, hardly believing his eyes. "It not fairy tale. It *real!*"

"I wish it was," Hank said. "It's only a copy. Even the stone isn't real. It's not a ruby. It's just a cheap imitation. Professor Orinaca at the university told me. The real dagger still hasn't been found."

From far below, Hank and Pedro heard a

church bell striking four o'clock. "Uh-oh, I go now!" cried Pedro. "Or I get in 'good' trouble! You need nothing, you call me?"

Hank said he would. After Pedro left, Hank felt all alone again. He lay down on the bed and fell asleep. He didn't know how long he had been asleep when the phone woke him up. "Mom?" he asked anxiously, answering the phone.

"No, Hank, I'm sorry. It's only Professor Orinaca," the voice on the other end of the line said.

"Hi, Professor," said Hank. "You sound weird, like the phones are different here."

"It's just a bad connection, Hank," said the professor. "Bolivian phones aren't as good as American ones, you know. That's why I might sound different. Is everything all right there?"

"Yeah, everything's fine. Have you heard from my mom yet?" Hank asked.

"No, I'm sorry." the professor said. "But something has come up. It's something about your father. I'd like you to be in on it. Bring the dagger. Meet me in 15 minutes, about 10 blocks from your hotel, at Sacarnaga and Linares. Ask a taxi driver, and he'll know the place. Can you make it?"

"I sure can!" Hank cried. "I'll be there, in 15 minutes!"

"Don't forget to bring the dagger," the professor reminded Hank, and then he hung up.

Hank grabbed the dagger from the bed and put it in his pocket. He took the elevator down to the lobby. He was almost out of the hotel when he heard a familiar voice calling to him.

"I can't stop now, Pedro," Hank told him, seeing his friend setting down some luggage at the check-in counter. "I'm going to meet the professor somewhere. He just called and said it's something about my father."

"Where you meet him?" Pedro asked, coming up to him as Hank started for the revolving door entrance to the hotel.

"He said Sacarnaga and Linares," Hank replied. "Are those street names?"

Pedro frowned. "Yes. But you know what's there?"

"No," Hank admitted. "I've never been in La Paz before. What *is* there?"

Pedro shook his head. "Bad news. That's *rinas*, the Witch Doctor's Market!"

"What's that?" asked Hank.

"It's an old, open-air market," Pedro said. "Indians sell magic potions and black magic dolls there. It's the center of all voodoo in the city!"

"Voodoo?" Hank asked. "The Indians still

really practice voodoo?"

"Some still do," Pedro admitted. "Most are Christians, but lots of people still like to mix in some black magic."

"Well, I have to go," said Hank slowly. "The professor called and told me to meet him there."

Pedro thought for a moment and then threw off his white hotel uniform jacket. "Tell you what, amigo. I go with!" he announced.

They were about to go out through the revolving doors when the desk clerk called out to Pedro. Hank could guess what he was saying, even though it was in Spanish.

Pedro came over to Hank, who was standing in the doorway. "I can't go, amigo. I lose my job."

Hank was disappointed, but said, "Hey, that's okay, Pedro. I'll see you later." After catching a taxi in front of the hotel in the hot afternoon sun, Hank rode through the city. In about 10 minutes, he was at the intersection of Sacarnaga and Linares streets. He paid the driver, and he got out and looked around.

He saw crowds of people gathered around stalls. Dark-skinned men and women who looked like gypsies were chanting and holding up beads and bunches of twigs and herbs. Some held little black-faced dolls.

Hank looked all around, but he didn't see Professor Orinaca. He decided to walk into the crowd of shoppers and tourists to see if the professor was at one of the stalls near the corner. Hank stared at the people in the stalls as they shouted out things in Spanish. Some called to him, but he waved his hand and walked on. An old Indian in a blanket and black hat jumped up in front of him and held out a bunch of weeds, saying, "Magic, magic."

Hank avoided him, and others like him, turning down alleys and ducking between stalls. The noise, smells, and strange sights began to make him feel dizzy. He wondered if he could find his way back to the corner where he was supposed to meet the professor.

Hank came to a stall that he thought he had passed on his way into the Witch Doctor's Market. He thought if he turned here, he'd be back at the intersection. He turned and began walking down the alley, trying to retrace his steps. But he soon found that instead of taking him out of the market, it took him deeper into it. There were hardly any people in this part of the market.

Finally, Hank found himself standing alone in front of a booth where a skinny old woman in rags was calling to him in a high-pitched, squeaky, Spanish voice. Hank heard a loud cackling screech that sounded like a crazy person laughing. He jumped back, startled. Peering into the dark of the booth, he saw a large white bird, like a parrot. Hank took a few steps backward.

The old woman took something out from under the blanket on her shoulders and held it out to Hank. It was one of those little black-faced dolls that he had seen at other stalls.

Suddenly, Hank knew what the doll was. It was a voodoo doll of death. Witches shape them into the likeness of a person they want dead. Then, they stick pins into the doll, and the person is supposed to die.

Hank heard a strange cry and turned around to run away from the old woman. He realized the strange sound he heard was his own voice. Before he could run more than a few steps, he felt a hand clamp over his mouth. Another hand clutched him around the waist and began dragging him into the shadows beside the old voodoo-seller's booth.

Hank couldn't cry out for help. Squirming and kicking, he could not free himself from the strong grasp of the man holding him.

All he could see of the man was the white sleeve of his suit coat.

CHAPTER 4

# *To the Rescue*

HANK felt himself being lifted off the ground. As lantern light fell among the shadows in an alley, he saw that Scarface was holding his legs, and the man in the white suit held him under the arms.

Twisting and turning, Hank tried to get free. The two men were carrying him to a car on a side street. The German lady sat in the driver's seat.

Just before the two men could dump him into the back seat of the car, Hank felt Scarface let go of his legs and fall to the alley. Then Hank saw a flash of something shiny and metallic crash down on the blond man's head. From out of nowhere, Pedro had grabbed a flagpole and had bashed the two men from behind.

Hank got to his feet and kicked Scarface in the shin. Pedro and Hank were shouting at the top of thier lungs, and that finally brought a crowd of people. The two men looked at the gathering crowd and made a run for it. Scarface ran for the car and got in it just moments before it pulled away. The blond man vanished in the alley.

Some people helped Pedro and Hank get up. Pedro explained that the men had tried to rob his American friend. A friendly man showed them the way out of the Witch Doctor's Market.

Back on the street again, Hank explained to Pedro what had happened. Hank felt his pocket. "The dagger!" he exclaimed. "It's gone! One of them must have stolen it while they carried me toward the car."

"But you say it was fake. Not worth nothing," Pedro said.

"They must not know that," Hank said, brushing the dust of the alley off himself. "I'm sure glad you followed me here," he said.

"Witch Doctor's Market no place for you alone. It's bad news, and I mean bad, not good," Pedro said with a laugh. "Let's get back to hotel. I tell desk clerk I have to go buy medicine for my sister. He wonder where I am."

"Well," Hank said, "*Gracias, amigo,* for coming to my rescue."

Back at the hotel, Hank found the professor waiting for him. Sitting in the hotel room, Hank told him what had happened.

"La Paz is full of thieves," the professor said. "You have to be very careful, Hank."

"But someone called me saying they were you. I was supposed to meet him at Witch Doctor's Market and to bring the dagger," Hank explained.

"I didn't call you," Orinaca said. "It sounds like someone knows you're in La Paz and have the dagger."

"They were the same people who tried to steal the box from me at the airport in Bogota," Hank told him.

"Well, I wouldn't worry about them anymore," Orinaca assured Hank. "Now they have the dagger, and they'll leave you alone."

"But how did they know I had the dagger?" Hank asked. "And who are these people?"

"The Dagger of Death seems to attract thieves," Orinaca explained, "and murderers. Leave everything to do with the dagger to me. It'll be safer for you."

"But Professor Orinaca," Hank protested, "my father disappeared while he was searching for the dagger! If I can get the real one, maybe it'll help lead us to him, and to my mother, too. I have to find them."

"They wouldn't want you to be in such danger," Orinaca insisted. "Many people who have searched for the Dagger of Death have met with terrible ends. You should not be among them."

"Look, Professor," Hank said desperately, "you're the only one who can help me, the only one I can trust. What if they were your parents? Could you just sit back and not do anything?"

Hank felt tears come to his eyes. He didn't want the professor to see him cry. But the more he thought about his parents possibly never coming back, the worse he felt. He wiped his eyes. "I just have to do everything I can to help my mom and dad. Let's start right away."

Orinaca took off his glasses and sighed. "I can tell you love your parents very much. Yes, I'll help you find them. But are you sure you want to go into the jungle? Why don't you stay here, where you're safe? The Bolivian jungle is a dangerous place, with wild animals and deadly snakes. We'll have to go through a region with some unfriendly natives. And what if your mother tries to get in touch with you?"

"She'd want me to be doing everything I can to help Dad. That's why she brought me along," argued Hank. "Besides, I have a feeling she's gotten mixed up in this dagger stuff, too. Maybe she's even with Dad."

"It will take a day or two to organize the expedition," Orinaca said. "In the meantime, I want you to keep out of trouble. You'd be safer if you stayed in the hotel."

"Okay," Hank agreed. "And Professor, there's one more thing. I'd like to take along my friend, Pedro. He's already helped me, and he'll be a big help on the search."

Orinaca hesitated for a moment, and then he said, "I guess one more person won't make much difference. But remember, this isn't going to be a picnic. He'll have to be very careful and do what I say."

"Thanks, Professor. That's just great!" Hank jumped up from the bed. "I'll go tell him now!" he cried.

Orinaca stood up. "Now, do me a favor, Hank. I've given in to you to take you and your friend along. All I ask is that you stay in the hotel until we leave. If, I mean, when we find your parents, I don't want to have to tell them something happened to you, all right?"

"It's a deal," Hank said.

The professor left, and Hank immediately went down to the lobby. He found Pedro and told him about the search expedition.

Pedro's big black eyes grew bigger with

excitement. "I get fired, but I go!" he exclaimed.

"But you can't lose your job. What about your family?" Hank asked.

Pedro thought a moment. "I fix it. I tell the manager, two of my sisters sick. Maybe one sick not enough. Two sick be enough. Maybe three?" he asked.

"Two ought to be enough," Hank suggested.

Pedro said "You not be sorry you take Pedro along. I know jungle. Like, how you say, 'back of my hand.' " He held up the backs of both hands to demonstrate. Then he frowned. "Jungles no fun. Bad snakes. Jaguar. Some Indians not friendly."

"I'm not afraid," Hank insisted.

Then Pedro ran his index finger slowly across his neck. "One more thing, Hank," Pedro said. "Headhunters in jungle!"

CHAPTER 5

# *A Walk in the Park*

THE next two days passed very slowly for Hank. He knew it took time to prepare an expedition. But it bothered him to sit around doing nothing but waiting when he was so anxious to help his parents. The phone didn't ring, and he couldn't get in touch with the professor at home or at the university. Of course, there was no word from his mother.

All the time alone with nothing to do left Hank a lot of time to think. And they weren't always happy thoughts. Lying on the bed in the hotel room, Hank worried about what would happen if they didn't find his mom and dad. Even though he tried not to think about the worst that could happen, terrible things still sometimes came into his mind. What would it be like to be an orphan? Where would he live? Who would he live with? He tried to push these thoughts out of his mind. He told himself that his father and mother weren't dead. He told himself that they were alive and were trying to find him, just as he was trying to find them.

Around noon on the second day, Pedro knocked on Hank's door. "Hey, amigo," he said, "time for lunch, no? How about you order us two cheeseburgers with everything? I go pick them up."

Twenty minutes later, the boys were sitting on the balcony enjoying their lunch.

"I think you should have ordered double everything," said Pedro as he finished off his french fries. "We have long trip ahead of us. No cheeseburgers in jungle."

Hank laughed. It felt good to joke. It took his mind off the dangerous parts of the journey they were about to start. "I don't know what you're talking about, Pedro," he said. "There are lots of restaurants in the jungle. We'll be able to get burgers whenever we want."

Pedro giggled. "Yeah, amigo. Alligator and crocodile burgers, maybe, or puma burgers. Mosquito burgers for sure!"

The boys laughed for a long time. It made Hank feel less nervous about the trip.

"So, Pedro," Hank said after a while. "Who are those headhunters you told me about?"

Hank asked, biting into a french fry.

"The Zi Xen," Pedro replied. "Not many left. They live hundreds of years ago in mountains of my country."

"They were very rich," Pedro went on. "But they sacrifice to the Sun God."

"With the Dagger of Death," Hank added.

"Sometimes animals, but mostly people," Pedro said. "People who come on their land, they get it. You know what I mean." Pedro moved his finger across his neck, like he did the other day.

"And they still live today in the area where we'll be going?"

"*Si,* Lake Titicaca. That's where the last of the Zi Xen live. High in the mountains, by the big lake."

"Whew," said Hank, "we'll have to be careful, eh amigo?"

"I take care of you. You take care of me. We be all right," said Pedro. "I go back to work now. See you later, alligator."

"Ughh," groaned Hank, "don't remind me!"

Hank sat on the balcony most of that afternoon, looking out over the city and at the mountains in the distance. Despite worry about the safety of his parents, despite fear of headhunters and wild animals, he was excited. He had been waiting all his life to go on an adventure like this. Stronger than everything else was the excitement of the expedition to start the next morning. It would lead him to danger, he was sure. But it would lead him to his parents, too. It would also lead him to the Dagger of Death.

Pedro returned to Hank's room after dinner and suggested that they take a walk in the park across the street from the hotel.

"You need to be in good shape," Pedro explained. "You sit around in hotel room all day, you not be able to walk in jungle."

Hank thought for a moment about Orinaca's warning to stay in the hotel. Then he decided that Pedro was right. He did need a little exercise. The boys crossed the street and entered the beautiful green park. They walked down long paths that were overgrown with vines and plants and strange flowers.

"So, how's your sick sister feeling?" Hank asked.

"That's sisters, amigo," Pedro replied. "They not good. Very sick. I think they be sick for many weeks, maybe months. No way to tell. I'm very worried."

The boys were laughing, when all of a sudden Hank told Pedro to be quiet.

"Look, Pedro," he whispered. "Over there by that tree."

"Hey, Hank! The *hombre* in the white suit." The boys ducked behind a bush.

"He hasn't seen us," Hank said. "Let's follow him. He may lead us to something."

"It's dangerous, amigo," said Pedro.

"We'll be careful, Pedro. Besides, danger is my middle name," said Hank with a devilish grin.

Pedro rolled his eyes at his friend.

The boys followed the man in the white suit down a winding path along high bushes and tall trees. Then the man took a turn across a large open space, where people were playing soccer. The boys darted behind bushes and soccer goalposts.

After following the man for about fifteen minutes, Hank began to feel uneasy. "Why do I get the feeling he's leading us somewhere?" Hank asked.

"You think he knows we're following him?"

Hank grew more certain the deeper they followed the man into the park. They were back in the woods now.

"It was too easy. He's wearing that white suit like a neon sign. I think he wanted us to see him. I bet he was hanging around the hotel waiting for us to come out. Now he's led us into the park."

Before Hank could any say more, the boys

realized they had lost sight of the man after he turned a curve in the path.

*Uh-oh,* thought Hank. *Where's he gone now?*

A moment later, Hank felt his arms pinned to his sides. A cloth gag was tied over his mouth and a blindfold placed over his eyes. Everything went dark. He tried to scream, but not a sound came out.

CHAPTER 6

# *A Drive in the Country*

HANK felt himself being carried a fairly long distance. Then he was thrown into a car. He couldn't see a thing, but he felt someone's leg next to his. He also heard the car radio playing what sounded like German polka music.

"Turn off that stupid cassette," he heard a rough voice say. The music stopped.

*Is Pedro here?* Hank wondered.

After the car had driven for few minutes, the same rough voice said, "Okay, kid, where's the real dagger? That one we got off you before was a fake. He should have told us."

*Who should have told you?*, Hank wondered. But he didn't have time to wonder long. Someone on his side grabbed the front of his shirt.

"We're tired of playing games with you, kid," a voice said. "You tell us where the real dagger is, or we'll feed you and your friend here to some hungry piranhas."

*You and your friend,* thought Hank. *That means Pedro's in the car somewhere.*

Hank heard the deep laughter of a woman in the driver's seat. He was sure it was the German woman from the airport.

Someone shook him from the side. "Talk kid, or something nasty will happen."

"Mmmmmnnnnppphhhhh," said Hank.

The rough voice from the front seat said, "Take that gag off, you idiot. He can't answer the question if he can't talk." Hank thought the rough voice sounded angry at the person next to him. The gag was removed.

"I don't know where the real dagger is!" Hank cried. "My father, Dr. Jeff Cooper, got lost looking for it in the jungle. Or, he found it, and someone is trying to get it away from him. Do you know where my father is?"

"Who cares about your father?" called the voice from the side, clutching the front of Hank's shirt again. Hank was sure it was the man in the white suit. "We know he planted the phony dagger in the Bogota airport. He told you where the real one is, didn't he? You tell us where it is, and maybe you'll see your father and mother again."

"How did you know the box at the airport

had the dagger in it?" Hank asked.

"Listen to him, asking *us* questions!" White Suit said.

The voice from the front seat that Hank thought had to be Scarface said, "I told you. The kid doesn't know where the dagger is. But, no, you're a smart guy. You keep saying he does, and you keep making us go through all this trouble. You know what could happen to us for kidnapping these two kids? The police will lock us up and throw away the key! I don't want to spend the rest of my life locked up in some crummy South American jail."

Hank was listening carefully to them argue. He figured that Scarface was smarter than White Suit. The German woman didn't say much of anything.

The three criminals seemed to know quite a bit, Hank realized. They knew about the dagger being in the box at the airport in Bogota. They knew his father had put it there. All they didn't know was that the dagger was a fake. And who was this someone who should have told them that? Who else was in on this hunt for the dagger? Who was this fourth person who seemed to be helping them?

"Don't talk to the kid anymore," Scarface said to White Suit. "He's already learned too much about our operation."

"*You* were the one who blabbed about not being told the dagger was a phony!" White Suit screamed. "I don't know why I got mixed up with you two creeps in the first place. I should have handled it myself."

Hank was beginning to feel better. It was obvious these people were amateurs, and not very smart ones either.

"Didn't I tell you to shut up, you lame-brained pretty boy?" Scarface shouted. "In another minute, you'll tell everything! I say we let these kids go. They don't know where the dagger is. We'll just get caught for kidnapping, and then it'll be all over for us."

"Who are you calling a pretty boy, you big fat slob?" shouted White Suit.

"Ah, be quiet, both of you," said the German woman from the front seat. "I'm sick of your bickering. I'm sick of this whole business."

Hank felt the car screech to a halt. The door opened, and he was roughly pushed out onto a road. Then he heard another person pushed out beside him. He heard the car tires squeal as the car drove away. "Bad boys!" the German woman shouted at them.

"Pedro, is that you? Are you okay?"

"Mmmmnnpphh," said Pedro.

"Let's work together to get these things off," said Hank. "Roll over here."

After a lot of work, they succeeded in getting Pedro's gag off. "Amigo, I only hear crickets," Pedro said. "We must be out in the country, no?"

"Listen. I hear a car. I hope the driver sees us here in the middle of the road," said Hank. "Scream as loud as you can!"

Hank heard the brakes of the oncoming car. He heard footsteps running toward them and excited voices shouting in Spanish. In a few moments the blindfolds were off, and their hands were untied.

* * * * *

"I tell you, amigo, I wanted to laugh!" Pedro told Hank when they were safely back at the hotel. "Those people crazy! They just about the dumbest crooks I ever see!"

"It's late, Pedro," Hank said and yawned. "It must be after one o'clock in the morning. We've got a big day ahead of us. We need to get some sleep."

Hank lay in his bed, listening to the night sounds of the city. But one thought kept running through his head, keeping him from falling asleep. *Who was this mysterious fourth person who was working with the three crooks to get the Dagger of Death?*

## CHAPTER 7
# *The Expedition Begins*

EARLY the next morning, Hank was hiding behind a large palm tree in the lobby of the hotel. Just a few yards away, Pedro was talking in Spanish to the desk clerk, his boss. Hank couldn't understand them, but he knew Pedro was explaining about his sick sisters. When Pedro held up three fingers, Hank thought, *Oh, no, I told him two sick sisters would be enough!*

Pedro stopped talking and looked down at the floor. The desk clerk frowned for a moment, and then he said something. Pedro grabbed the man's hand and shook it happily and then ran off. When he passed the palm that Hank was hiding behind, he gave him a thumbs-up. Hank followed Pedro down a hallway where the desk clerk couldn't see them.

"I be back right away. I need to get some

things for the trip," Pedro shouted and ran out a side entrance to the hotel. *What could be so important,* Hank wondered returning to his room to finish packing. The professor was going to pick them up in an hour.

After finishing his packing, Hank lay on the bed and thought about the trip ahead. He thought about all the times he had wished he could go with his parents on one of their adventures. He never dreamed he would be going on one under these conditions. Would this adventure lead to his father? Would it lead to the Dagger of Death? What was in store for him at the end of this journey?

His thoughts were interrupted by Pedro as he burst into the room. "Okay, amigo!" he shouted joyfully. "Now we ready for anything!"

Pedro tossed his now full backpack on the bed and started to show Hank what he had brought. First, he pulled out two cans of insect spray.

Hank laughed. "Do you think this stuff will keep away jaguars and headhunters?"

"Oh, sure," answered Pedro, "no problem. Just use a lot of it."

In Pedro's pack were also several packs of bubble gum, some candy, a soccer ball, some firecrackers and small rockets.

"What's all this stuff for?" asked Hank.

"You'll have to carry it, you know."

"We want a little fun after long day on the trail, no?" Pedro answered.

Laughing, Hank said, "Okay, but that soccer ball's too big. That stays behind. Besides, we're going into the jungle. Where would we play?"

They were interrupted by the telephone. Hank answered to find that it was Professor Orinaca calling from the lobby to say he was ready to go.

In the taxi cab, Orinaca explained to the boys, "We'll fly to a village about 100 miles from here, high in the Andes. There we'll join our guide. He'll take us to Lake Titicaca."

Hank stared out the cab window, watching the city. *When will be the next time I see La Paz?* he wondered.

"Remember, boys," continued the professor, "this isn't going to be any picnic. We'll be hacking our way through thick jungle and crossing streams with crocodile and piranha. We may meet up with Indians who don't like strangers coming into their territory. I'm not trying to scare you, but I just want you to know what we're in for. It's not too late to turn around and go back to the hotel."

Hank and Pedro exchanged looks and smiled.

"No way, Professor," said Hank firmly. "We're both going."

At the airport, they boarded a small, single-engine plane that looked to Hank like it had been built by the Wright Brothers. Hank noticed as he sat in his seat waiting for the plane to take off that Pedro was white as a sheet.

"Hey, amigo!" Hank shouted above the noise of the rickety old plane. "Don't worry. This thing'll fly okay, I hope." Pedro was too scared to speak. Hank realized that, of course, Pedro had never been up in an airplane before.

With a tremendous shaking and a loud roar, the old plane finally took off. Soon, they were away from the city, and Hank looked down to see a thick carpet of green as far as the horizon. The snow-capped Andes Mountains were just ahead.

Pedro had finally gotten up the courage to look out the window. Hank was pointing out a tall mountain just ahead.

"I hope the bottom of the plane no scrape the mountain," was all Pedro said.

The engine began coughing, and the plane hit an air pocket. Hank and Pedro both grabbed their armrests. Hank looked at his friend.

"I've flown in this plane before," Orinaca told the boys. "She may be old, but she's okay. She'll get us where we want to go."

Hank hoped the professor was right. Pedro forced his eyes straight ahead and would not look down.

Looking out the window, Hank saw forests and fields spread out below in every direction. Sometimes he saw winding blue rivers and streams coming down out of the mountains. Once in a while, he saw a small village along a riverbank, with clusters of huts and a few people and cows and goats walking around. The farther the plane flew, the fewer villages and people he saw.

"We're getting pretty far from civilization now," Hank said to the professor in the seat in front of him.

"The next village is an hour away," Orinaca told him. "We'll land there and join our guide."

"It's okay, Pedro," Hank said. "We're almost there. Then you can breathe again."

"I breathe when we hit the ground, not before," Pedro said without turning his head.

About an hour passed, and Hank noticed the pilot was bringing the plane down. Below he saw only more jungle, with a wide, blue-green river winding through it. Then, ahead, he saw a small open field and a village nearby of about a dozen huts. *Not much of a landing strip,* he thought.

But the pilot brought the plane down smoothly, and soon the passengers got out and stretched their legs.

"There, that wasn't so bad, was it?" Hank asked Pedro. But Pedro didn't answer. He was down on his knees kissing the dirt.

Professor Orinaca led the way to the cluster of huts beside the riverbank. There were lots of Indians arranging boxes and supplies. Ordering them around was one of the biggest men Hank had ever seen. The man was wearing a safari outfit like Orinaca's. He also had a colorful shawl that the Indians called a serape over his shoulders and a black derby hat that Hank had seen on many Indians.

"It's good to see you again, Coatibamba," Professor Orinaca said, shaking the Indian's hand. Then he introduced Hank and Pedro.

"No like having boys along," Coatibamba said in a stern, deep voice that nearly shook the ground under Hank and Pedro. "Better behave. No trouble, or feed you to piranha."

Professor Orinaca whispered to Hank. "He's only joking."

"Yeah, I bet," Hank said under his breath to Pedro.

"We must get started soon," Coatibamba

announced. "Long way to Lake Titicaca. Wish not going. Had bad dream last night."

Pedro, who had gotten his breath and courage back, explained to Hank. "Witch doctor explain his dream for him. Maybe he say Coatibamba's future not so good. Hope ours is better."

Witch doctors interpreting dreams sounded kind of crazy to Hank. He began to wonder about their guide. Coatibamba looked like Samson. He was so big and strong. But if he believed in dreams and witch doctors, maybe he wasn't so smart.

"We go through the Caranavi," Coatibamba was telling the professor.

"The Caranavi? What's that?" Hank asked the professor.

"It's a tropical area of dense rain forest high in these mountains," Orinaca explained. "Some of the most beautiful and spectacular waterfalls in all of Bolivia are there. But there are crocodiles, piranha, wild animals, and some Indian tribes that are often unfriendly to outsiders. We have to travel through the Caranavi to get to Lake Titicaca and the island of the Zi Xen. I told you it wasn't going to be a Sunday walk in the park."

Coatibamba motioned for them to follow, and they marched along behind him.

"Coatibamba's people have lived in these mountains a thousand years," Professor Orinaca told Hank. "They lived here before Columbus came to America. He knows the jungles, and he's the best guide in these parts. But he's tight-lipped, unless he doesn't like something or someone. Then you know about it."

"He doesn't like me or Pedro very much, I can tell," Hank said.

They followed as Coatibamba led them to the riverbank at the edge of the small village.

"Just stay out of his way, and do what he tells you," Orinaca cautioned.

They joined up with half a dozen other dark-skinned natives who carried tents, food, and other supplies for the trip on their backs. Coatibamba led them single-file into the jungle. Almost immediately, he began hacking away at the dense jungle with a machete. It was the meanest piece of steel Hank had ever seen. He saw how it sliced through even the thickest rope-like tree branches that blocked their path. Behind him, the other natives used their machetes to clear the way for the professor and the two boys, who brought up the rear.

Hours passed slowly as the heat of the day turned the jungle into a steam bath. Sweat poured off Hank's forehead and soaked his clothes. Flies and mosquitos swarmed around him. Overhead, he heard birds squawking and screeching in weird voices. More than once he saw long, fat snakes slithering around in the trees. Coatibamba said they were anacondas or boa constrictors.

Just about the time Hank thought he would drop from exhaustion, Coatibamba stopped and held up a hand.

"We camp here tonight," he announced. Then he gave his men some orders. Some began pitching tents while others began building a fire.

Coatibamba took a long spear down to the river. Hank watched with Pedro from a limb high in a tree as their guide speared some big blue fish for their dinner. It tasted delicious fried over the open fire that night with some fresh vegetables the Indians had carried in their packs. For dessert, they ate blackberries that Coatibamba saw growing in the jungle near their camp.

"Only eat from jungle what I say is okay," Coatibamba cautioned the boys. "Some things that grow here are poisonous."

Hank yawned. He and Pedro were both very tired after hours of walking in the jungle heat, and their tent looked good to them.

Pedro entered the tent first. Before Hank could follow him in, Professor Orinaca called to him.

"I'd like to show you something, Hank, before you turn in," the professor told him and motioned for him to follow.

Hank wondered what Orinaca wanted to show him, and he was almost too tired to follow. The professor led him away from the camp, up the mountainside. In the bright glow of a half moon, Orinaca led Hank up a mountain path to the top of a cliff. The professor spread out his arm to show Hank the spectacular view.

From high up on the mountain, Hank looked out over the winding river that cut through the jungle far below, and he saw the water shimmering in the moonlight. Birds sang in the trees around them, and creatures in the jungle chattered playfully.

"It's beautiful," Hank said. He thought he had never seen country so beautiful. "Thanks for bringing me up here, Professor."

"I didn't want you to miss this sight," Orinaca said, putting an arm around Hank's shoulder. "I'll never forget the time I showed it to your father and mother. It was on the expedition in that photo I keep on my desk."

Hearing that made Hank feel good. Now

he was standing on the very spot where his mother and father had stood. It made him feel closer to them. He missed them more than ever that night.

Would he find them soon, or...?

Clouds began to cover the moon. Orinaca suggested they go back down to the camp before it grew too dark.

"Be careful of your footing," the professor cautioned Hank as he led the way down the steep mountain path.

Dark clouds moved over the moon, and for a moment Hank could not see the path ahead clearly. He tried following the professor, but Orinaca had gone a little ahead of him. Hank had to scramble to keep up.

Suddenly, the ground beneath his hiking boots crumbled as Hank walked close to the edge of the mountain path. He felt himself falling. Spreading out beneath him, he saw the entire Caranavi valley and the river far below.

Hank reached out for a branch or vine to grab onto, but he found nothing within his grasp. Crying out for help, he felt himself sliding farther down the mountainside.

After what seemed like several long minutes, Hank's fall stopped. He found himself on a tiny ledge, overlooking the valley. Stones and clumps of dirt were knocked loose, and they tumbled down the side of the mountain.

"Help!" he called out. "I'm on a ledge out here!"

Looking up, Hank saw Professor Orinaca. He was looking down at him from the mountain path. The ledge beneath Hank began to crumble again.

*What are you waiting for?* Hank wondered. "Help!" he cried out again. "Help! I'm falling!"

CHAPTER 8

# *A Visitor in the Night*

HANK couldn't see the professor when he looked up again. *Where is he?!?!* went through Hank's mind. *Why won't he help me?* Hank felt the ground giving way under his feet. He dug his fingers into the rock wall of the cliff ledge, but there was nothing to hold on to. One foot slipped off the ledge, and Hank screamed.

Then, out of nowhere, he saw Coatibamba. The guide was leaning down to Hank from a tree that hung out over the side of the mountain.

"Take hold. I pull you up!" Coatibamba roared. Reaching for his life, Hank's fingers met Coatibamba's. He felt the guide grab his hand firmly and begin to pull him up. Moments later, the ledge collapsed. Dirt and rocks crashed down the mountainside to the valley far below.

In the wink of an eye, Hank found himself standing safely beside the huge guide who had saved his life.

"What were you doing way out there?" Coatibamba asked while Hank caught his breath and tried to stop trembling.

"Professor Orinaca and I..." he said between gasps for air. "He brought me up here to show me the view."

Coatibamba looked around in the darkness of the night as clouds covered the moon. "Orinaca? Where is he?"

"Here I am," Orinaca said, as he came toward them from out of the jungle. "I tried coming down to rescue you, Hank, but I slipped myself. If I hadn't found a vine to grab hold of, I would have gone off a ledge myself. Are you all right, Hank?" He put his arm around Hank.

"I'm fine, Professor," answered Hank. "I'm just a little out of breath." *Why didn't you help me?* Hank thought.

"Well, thank goodness you're safe," Orinaca said, helping Hank down the mountain path to the camp.

Coatibamba said nothing as they walked back to camp. Hank could see his face lost in thought when the moon came out from behind a cloud.

When he got back to his tent, Hank saw that Pedro was already fast asleep. He decided to wait until morning to tell him about his near escape.

When Hank awoke the next morning, he was shivering from the cold. The temperature had fallen enough overnight for snow to collect on the ground. Hank could hardly believe it when he opened his tent and looked out.

"Here, put this on," Pedro said behind him, tossing Hank something that looked like a woolen blanket, just like the one Coatibamba had worn the day before. "It's a serape," said Pedro. "Snow will melt fast, and it get hot again."

Hank put on his long pants and shirt, and then he pulled the serape on over his head. He felt warm again under the serape. Hank told Pedro about his brush with death the night before.

"I still can't figure it out," Hank said, remembering. "Orinaca was close enough to pull me up. But he just stood there looking down at me, like he couldn't decide whether to help me or not. I know it sounds crazy, but there was something weird in his eyes. It gave me the creeps."

"What was it?" Pedro asked.

Hank thought about it another moment. "I

don't know, Pedro. I just don't know."

"I thought you say he a good friend of your *padre*."

"He says he is," Hank said, lacing up his hiking boots. "And Dad says so, too. So I don't get it. Why would he look at me like he did, and not come down to help me? In another minute, I'd have been a goner."

"What is 'goner'?" asked Pedro.

Hank smiled. "You know," he answered running his finger across his neck like Pedro had done earlier. "Dead."

"Well, I'm glad Coatibamba save you. So you not be goner." Pedro put a friendly hand on Hank's shoulder, and then he scrambled under him for his own boots. "He not say much, but he okay."

After a breakfast of beans and tortillas that Hank barely touched, the expedition started on its way again. Pedro had been right. After the sun was up an hour, the snow melted, and the green of the jungle and plains returned. So did the mounting heat. So, off went the serapes, and on went short pants.

Hank had to laugh at Pedro. He had traded some bubble gum for one of the black derby hats that the guides wore. Pedro looked funny in it. Hank preferred his Chicago Bears cap, which all the Indians admired.

The morning passed pretty uneventfully as Coatibamba led the group deeper into the jungle, hacking away with his machete to open a path. As usual, Orinaca followed behind Coatibamba, and after him came the Indians, carrying the supplies. Hank and Pedro were last in the line.

They wound along the banks of a narrow, blue river where the water whipped up into whitecaps as it rushed over large stones and boulders. Later that morning, Coatibamba stopped for a moment to listen to a sound. One of the Indians cried out, "Jaguar!"

Hank watched as Coatibamba shaded his eyes from the sun to peer into the jungle ahead of them. While the others were looking that way for the jaguar, Hank heard sounds like branches breaking behind them in the bush.

*What's moving in the trees?* he wondered. Then he saw what had made the noise. It wasn't a jaguar, but two men, almost hidden among the vines and bushes about 30 yards behind them.

First he recognized Scarface, and then White Suit. After catching sight of them for just a second, they disappeared back into the dense jungle.

He told Pedro, but his friend said he hadn't

seen them. Pedro had been busy looking at Coatibamba trying to see the jaguar. Coatibamba raised a hand and told everyone to continue onward. "Jaguar not hungry for us. Eating young puma. Okay to go on."

Hank didn't think the jaguar looked all that safe to pass by, but he followed as the procession went on.

Hank had other worries. Should he tell the professor or anyone else that he saw Scarface and White Suit? He wasn't sure he could trust Orinaca anymore, in spite of what his mother had said.

Hank decided to be like Coatibamba, tight-lipped. He would keep a watch out for the two men lurking behind them in the jungle, and he would only let Pedro in on it. He had a pretty good idea why Scarface and White Suit were following them. They were following the expedition, hoping it would lead them to the Dagger of Death. Hank thought that if they were willing to follow them this far into the jungle, they were probably willing to do anything to get the dagger.

Half an hour later, the sun was overhead, and Coatibamba held up a hand to stop them again. They were at a bend in the river where Coatibamba said the fishing was good. Hank was glad to stop at last, but he wasn't looking forward to a lunch of more fish. He'd rather have Pedro bring them a couple of room-service cheeseburgers.

After their lunch, a strong, cold wind began blowing. On went the serapes and long pants.

"I think *surazo* coming," Coatibamba cautioned.

Pedro explained, "*Surazo* a wind. Strong, cold, blowing from Antarctic. Bring bad rainstorms."

In less than an hour, the weather had turned from hot and humid with almost no breeze to cold and windy. Dark clouds gathered overhead, and thunder began to rumble around them.

Soon the rains came. Hank and Pedro sat in their tent as the wild, angry storm crashed around them. After a while, water began to seep into the floor of their tent. Shivering under his serape, Hank felt miserable.

"Hey, amigo," said Pedro cheerfully. "Professor say trip be no picnic. Want bubble gum?"

Hank shook his head. Nothing seemed to get Pedro down. Not even sitting in a wet tent in the middle of the jungle with jaguars and snakes prowling all around them.

Hours later, when the storm had blown over, someone opened the flap of their tent.

"Are you boys all right," asked Professor Orinaca. "That was a pretty bad storm."

Hank said they were wet but fine. He wondered why Orinaca seemed so concerned for them now. He didn't seem to be very concerned when Hank was hanging on the ledge.

"Good," said the professor, putting his hand on Hank's shoulder. "Coatibamba says we'll camp here for the night." Hank didn't feel comforted by the professor's hand on his shoulder, not after what had happened. He had a strange feeling about the man that nothing could get rid of. Hank decided to be on his guard.

At dinner that night, Orinaca seemed to change. Up until then, he had been almost as tight-lipped as Coatibamba. After looking in on Hank after the *surazo* passed, the professor seemed more cheerful. Hank decided to keep his eye on him.

Night fell fast, and cold winds blew down again from the snow-capped mountains. Hank and Pedro sat up late by the camp fire, after the professor went to his tent. Pedro asked Hank if he knew any ghost stories. Hank told Pedro a scary tale that he had learned on a Boy Scout camping trip. When he was finishing his story, he saw someone moving in the shadows around them

He watched while he finished his story, but he could not see who it was. Then, after a few moments, he saw Coatibamba motioning for them to follow him.

Coatibamba stepped back behind a tree and waited for them to join him. They walked some distance out into the jungle together, before Coatibamba spoke.

"I see you at fire but not sit with you to talk," Coatibamba said in a low voice. "Professor would see."

Hank stared at the guide's brown face.

"Coatibamba wait 'til now to warn you," the guide said softly, frowning. "Not sure before, but more sure now."

"Warn me?" Hank asked. "About what?"

"Orinaca," Coatibamba said. "Do not trust him."

"I had the feeling I shouldn't trust him," Hank said, "but why do you say I shouldn't?"

"Listen," the guide said. "On last expedition, I hear Jeff Cooper and Orinaca argue in tent one night. Coatibamba not know what they argue about, but Orinaca say mean words. He not like your father."

"I thought they were good friends," Hank said.

"They were, once. But now, no," said the

guide. "Then I see how Orinaca look at you, from start of expedition. He no like you, either. Last night, I think he wish you fall. He no help you."

"I got the same feeling," Hank admitted.

"So, I warn you," Coatibamba said, getting up. "I try be around, to keep you and friend safe. But not be around always. Maybe need to keep myself safe, too. Orinaca not like me, either. But I have this to protect me. You not have."

Coatibamba held up his machete. Hank thought about how easily it sliced through the thick vines on the trail, and felt that anyone who messed with Coatibamba would be in big trouble.

Hank remembered something. He decided to tell Coatibamba, who seemed to be their new friend, about seeing Scarface and White Suit lurking behind them in the jungle earlier that day. Then he explained his run-ins with them back in Bogota and La Paz.

"I know them," Coatibamba replied, shaking his head. "Have had trouble with them before. They like jackals. They follow expeditions, to steal from rich people on safari."

"But we're not rich. Why are they following us?" Hank asked, wondering if Coatibamba had the same answer as he had.

Coatibamba looked hard at Hank. "I know why you go to Lake Titicaca," he said. "Look for your father and Dagger of Death. Those two men know, too. They follow us on last expedition."

"You led my father on the expedition to find the dagger!" Hank cried, starting to piece things together. "You were there when he disappeared!"

"Yes," Coatibamba said. "Orinaca on expedition, too."

"Where is my father now? Do you know, Coatibamba?" Hank asked excitedly. "Is he alive? What happened to him?"

Coatibamba shook his head. "He disappear. That part is true. We on Isla del Sol in Lake Titicaca, then no see him anymore. We search for days. Then Professor say we stop and go home."

"So, it was Orinaca who gave up the search," Hank said.

"I want keep looking," Coatibamba said. "Jeff Cooper was good man. He always good to Coatibamba. Not like Orinaca. Orinaca cheap and mean. But Orinaca say stop search, and I have to stop and take him back out of jungle."

"Did my father find the Dagger of Death?" Hank asked anxiously.

"Not know. Coatibamba not see him find the Dagger of Death, but maybe found it."

"So, you last saw him on Isla del Sol in Lake Titicaca," Hank confirmed.

"We look there for ruins of Zi Xen civilization," the guide said. "Not find, then look, and your father not with us."

"Do you think he's still alive?" Hank held his breath waiting for the guide's reply.

"Bad country," Coatibamba said. "Zi Xen take heads of strangers who enter their jungle. They look for dagger, too. It sacred to them. They cut off head of men who come search for Dagger of Death before."

The three of them sat in silence for a moment. Then Coatibamba stood up and said, "I go now, or Orinaca look for me. Remember. Coatibamba warn you. Not trust Orinaca."

After the guide left their tent, Pedro looked at Hank. "So you right about Orinaca," said Pedro.

"I feel better, knowing Coatibamba seems to want to help us," Hank replied, shivering again under his serape as the night grew colder.

But it wasn't only the falling temperature and the snow that sent a cold chill through him. It was the thought of all the dangers that he knew surrounded him. He thought of Orinaca in his tent near theirs, and of Scarface and White Suit lurking outside in the jungle. And he could not get his mind off of the Zi Xen. Were they hunting his father's head, and maybe his mother's, too? Could they even be hunting his?

CHAPTER 9

# *Lake Titicaca and the Isla del Sol*

SOMETIME in the dark of early morning, Hank awoke from a nightmare that left him in a sweat. He dreamed that a jaguar was chasing him from one direction, while from another direction a Zi Xen was coming at him with a machete to cut off his head.

Hank tried to calm himself by thinking about what he would be doing if he were back home in Chicago. He thought he would be with his friends that afternoon at a Cubs baseball game. He thought about how different the jungles of Bolivia were from his life back home. He fell off to sleep again with a picture of himself sitting in the sun high up in the bleachers at Wrigley Field.

Coatibamba had good news for them at breakfast.

"This afternoon, we reach Lake Titicaca," he announced. "Still long way ahead. But before dark, we be there."

As the expedition continued through the jungle, Hank kept looking around for any new sign of Scarface or White Suit. Hank suspected that the two men had patched up their falling out. He knew only one thing could make them do that...the hope of finding the Dagger of Death.

Before starting off again, Coatibamba warned everyone that they were approaching Zi Xen territory. It was wilder jungle, with more dangerous animals. There were puma, wildcat, and jaguar. And the rivers held not only alligator, crocodile, and piranha, but also the deadly caiman. But that morning, all they heard or saw were monkeys chattering in the trees above them and the strange cries of the tropical birds.

Hank felt that each step took him closer to solving the mystery of what had happened to his father. What would he find out? Approaching Lake Titicaca meant they were getting closer to the place where his father had last been seen. Thoughts like these filled Hank's mind during the long, hard hike that day.

In late afternoon, under a blazing sun and in stifling heat, Coatibamba called to them from the front of the expedition, "It's Lake Titicaca!"

Hank and Pedro ran ahead, even though they were dead tired, and they stood next to Coatibamba. Together they gazed at the blue water. The lake was larger than Hank had imagined, and even more beautiful. In the middle of the lake were green islands that looked like they were floating.

Hank threw off his backpack and clothes, and dived into the lake. He came up for air and shouted, "It's freezing!"

Coatibamba, laughing on shore as he watched, told him, "Lake is always cold. Even on hottest day. It is so deep and so high in the mountains."

Pedro threw off his clothes and found a vine to swing from. He dropped into the lake next to Hank. While the boys swam, Coatibamba and his men began building reed boats to take them out to Isla del Sol.

Later that afternoon, the boys rode in Coatibamba's boat toward a cluster of islands. After passing several smaller islands on the way, Coatibamba pointed to a larger island.

"My name comes from that island," he said. "Coati, the Island of the Moon. Many ruins there, of old tribe."

It made Hank more eager than ever to keep going and reach the Island of the Sun that he saw stretching out ahead on the lake, the largest island on Lake Titicaca.

About an hour later, Coatibamba beached their boat in a cove. They stepped ashore onto Isla del Sol. While they looked around on the rocky forested shore, the others pulled their boats onto the shore.

Standing on the shore of Isla del Sol, Hank felt like he had taken another big step toward solving the mystery of his father's disappearance, and maybe his mother's disappearance, too. For a moment, he looked behind him on the lake, and wondered about Scarface and White Suit. Where were they now? Had they built boats and even followed them here, across the lake?

Professor Orinaca looked more excited than he had since the trip began. Hank could guess why.

"We must be careful now," Coatibamba cautioned everyone. "I know Zi Xen. Remember that they take the heads of strangers. We look for Jeff Cooper, not dagger."

Hank watched Orinaca carefully when Coatibamba mentioned the Dagger of Death.

"Maybe we'll be lucky," Orinaca said. "Maybe we'll find Dr. Cooper and the dagger."

Hank had a feeling which one was more important to the professor. "But, of course,"

Orinaca said quickly, "it's most important that we find Jeff Cooper."

Coatibamba urged them to start their search of the island. Hank soon realized that the island was not only bigger than he imagined, but more rugged. It was like the mainland, with high mountains and deep valleys, and it was all densely forested. Once they left the shore, the high trees blocked out any view of the lake. The deeper they went into the island's jungle, the less like an island it became.

With every step the Indians took, they looked and listened for any sign of Zi Xen. Hank could see their growing sense of fear. Hank and Pedro also became more tense and alert.

Just when Hank and Pedro felt they couldn't take another step, Coatibamba put up his hand. "Make camp here for the night," said the guide.

After another fish dinner and some time around the camp fire, Coatibamba assigned some of the Indians to stand guard. They were to warn the others if there was any sign of the Zi Xen.

Even with the guards, Hank was too anxious to sleep. Again he tossed and turned, long after Pedro had fallen asleep. Nothing seemed to keep Pedro from falling asleep.

Hank heard monkeys chattering in the trees around the camp. Usually the monkeys were quiet this time of night. He wondered why they were making noise now. Was Orinaca wandering around? Had Scarface and White Suit followed them in a boat to the island? Was a jaguar or puma stalking through the underbrush around the camp? Or, were some Zi Xen standing outside his tent looking for some heads?

Hank finally fell asleep. He awoke later and thought he heard a strange sound in the jungle. Looking out of his tent, he saw the black sky full of stars. Then Hank looked toward the camp fire. He was surprised to see no one standing there. *What's going on? Where are the guards?* he wondered. Hank climbed out of his tent and looked around. He didn't see any of the guards. He walked quickly over to Coatibamba's tent, but the guide was not there.

Hank checked Professor Orinaca's tent next, but it too was empty. Hank began to feel panicky as he checked the tents, one by one, and found them empty.

He ran back to his tent, half-expecting to find it empty as well. But there Pedro was, fast asleep. Hank quickly woke up Pedro and told him that they were alone in the camp.

Pedro yawned and tried to understand what Hank was telling him.

"What you mean, alone?" Pedro asked, blinking and trying to wake up. "It morning yet?"

"No, it's still night, and everyone's gone," Hank told him.

"Where everyone go?" Pedro asked.

"Shhh! What's that sound?" Hank asked in a whisper. He put a finger to his lips to tell Pedro to be quiet for a moment. They both listened.

Far off in the jungle, they heard a low chanting, like the sound of men singing a strange song. And the chanting was coming closer.

## CHAPTER 10
# *A Familiar Face*

"WE'RE not safe in the tent," whispered Hank. "Get dressed, and let's get out of here. We'll hide in the jungle." Pedro followed Hank out into the brush and jungle.

Through openings in the trees, Hank and Pedro saw several Indians. "Those aren't Coatibamba's men," whispered Hank. These men were nearly naked. Their skin was darker, and as they came closer, Hank saw that they had painted themselves. They were taller than Coatibamba's men, and they carried spears and bows and arrows. They walked around the camp looking into the tents.

Then Hank saw a line of more Indians coming out of the jungle into the camp fire area. They were leading someone he recognized.

It was Coatibamba, his hands tied behind him as he was pushed along. Behind him followed his men, who were also tied up. Hank pointed toward Coatibamba, and Pedro looked and nodded.

"Must be Zi Xen," whispered Pedro.

Hank knew it was true.

Hank wondered where Professor Orinaca was. Had he been killed by the natives? Had he escaped into the jungle like he and Pedro. Then, Hank saw something that almost made his heart stop.

One of the Indians ran into the light of the camp fire holding a machete in one hand and something round and black in the other. The Indian was holding up a human head.

As the Indian danced closer to the light of the fire, Hank saw that the head was Scarface's!

"That one has Scarface's knife," Pedro whispered and pointed to another Zi Xen.

Suddenly, Hank felt a hand grab his arm.

Expecting to see another Zi Xen behind him with his machete raised to cut off his head, Hank closed his eyes.

Instead of a blood-curdling scream, Hank heard whimpering and crying. He opened his eyes to see White Suit standing next to him.

Hank hardly recognized him. His white suit was torn and filthy, and he was scratched, dirty, and bleeding.

"They killed Morrison!" he kept repeating to Hank and Pedro. "They almost got my head, but I got away!" He was hysterical, and Hank tried to keep him quiet. "Look," Hank said. "Calm down, and be quiet. Or they'll hear you. Then we'll all be done for!"

White Suit grabbed Hank by the arms and began pleading with him. "Don't let them kill me! Give them anything. If you have the Dagger of Death, give it to them, or they'll cut off *all* our heads!"

*Luckily,* Hank thought, *the Zi Xen hadn't heard them over their own chanting and shouting.*

"Let's get away from them," Hank whispered to the others. They went further back into the jungle, all the while keeping an eye on the Zi Xen. They came to a higher spot that overlooked the campsite, and they could see the Zi Xen dancing in the firelight. To their relief, Hank, Pedro, and White Suit saw that Coatibamba and his men hadn't been harmed. The Zi Xen were chanting and dancing around the one who held the head of Scarface, or Morrison. They seemed to be ignoring Coatibamba and his men.

When they were safely away from the Zi Xen, Hank asked, "Who are you?"

White Suit had calmed down enough to talk,

but he was still frightened by what he had seen.

"I wish I'd never met Morrison or Helga and gotten mixed up in this Dagger of Death business," he moaned.

"I'm an Englishman. My name's Knowles," the man continued. "I came here to South America after I got into a little trouble in England. About a year ago, I ran into Jack Morrison in La Paz. We started working together, and now some Indian is holding his head. And mine's probably going to be next."

"But what about the Dagger of Death? And my father? Do you know where he is?"

The man kept looking in the direction of the camp fire. Hank could see the firelight reflected in Knowles' frightened eyes.

"It doesn't look like we're going to get out of here alive, so I might as well tell you," said Knowles. "Morrison and the German woman, Helga Schmidt, were partners in La Paz. Her job was to find out for Morrison when expeditions into the jungle started. Then he'd follow the expedition and rob the rich people out in the jungle. When Helga learned that your dad was going into the jungle to look for the Dagger of Death, she told Morrison about it. He needed a man to help him, so they asked me. I didn't have anything better to do, so I agreed to go." Knowles looked toward the firelight. "I would have been better off if I'd stayed where I was."

"But how did Helga Schmidt learn that my father was going to search for the dagger?" Hank asked.

"It was that rat Orinaca," Knowles replied in an angry voice. "He was looking for someone to get the dagger from your father. He knew Helga could find people to steal valuables. He told her he would pay her, if she helped him get the dagger."

Hank began to put the pieces together. "So, Orinaca sent you and Morrison and Helga to Bogota to steal the package."

Knowles nodded.

"How did Orinaca know the dagger was in the box at the airport in Bogota?" Hank asked.

"Search me," said Knowles. "All I know now is that Orinaca thought the box contained the real dagger. Later, he tried to pull a fast one on Morrison and Helga and me."

Hank guessed the rest. "When Orinaca found out the dagger was only a copy, he didn't tell you or the others. But why not?"

"He paid us off after we got back to La Paz and said that you got away with the box. He said he didn't need us anymore."

Hank put more of the pieces together.

"Orinaca didn't tell you that he'd gotten the dagger from me and discovered it was a phony. So, you thought I still had the real dagger."

"I called you at the hotel, pretending I was Orinaca," Knowles admitted, "to lure you to Witch Doctor's Market."

"But why didn't you give up after taking the fake dagger from me at the market?" Hank asked. "Didn't you know it was a fake?"

"Yeah, we knew," Knowles answered. "Helga had someone check it out, and they told us it was just a copy. But you were our only link to finding the real one, so Morrison and Helga talked me into grabbing you in the park. After that, I got fed up with them and split."

"But what are you doing here, if you split with them?" Hank asked.

"Ah, Morrison talked me into it. He kept telling me stories about how we'd be millionaires after we had the dagger," Knowles said, shaking his head. There were beads of sweat on his forehead. "Now someone's dancing around a fire, holding his head, and I'm up here, waiting for someone to cut mine off."

"So, you three decided that you didn't need Orinaca, after he'd paid you off," Hank said. "You'd find the dagger yourselves and not share it with the professor."

"You got it, kid," Knowles said. "I'll tell you what. If you find that dagger, do me a favor, and keep it. Anyone who has it is going to get his head cut off!"

"Where the professor now?" Pedro asked Knowles.

"I don't know where he is," Knowles answered. "Morrison and I were by ourselves in the jungle, waiting for you to break camp in the morning so we could follow you. Some headhunters jumped us. Morrison punched the chief, and they killed him. You see where he is now." Knowles nodded toward the dancing Indians by the campfire. "They were going to get me next, but some Indian ran up, talking excitedly about your expedition. I got away in the excitement. I went back to the beach for the boat we left there, but it was gone. All the boats are gone. Yours is too."

"So, you came back to the camp and found that the Zi Xen had taken everyone prisoner, except Orinaca," Hank said.

"The Zi Xen trust him, the fools," Knowles said. "They think he'll find the dagger and give it back to them. I know him better than that. He'd risk his head for the dagger any day."

*Orinaca must want the Dagger of Death*

*pretty badly to try to work a deal with the Zi Xen,* Hank thought. *It was risky business. The professor must figure selling the dagger would be worth it.*

Knowles stood up. "You can stay here and get caught if you want," he told the boys. "I'm going to find myself one of those boats and get off this island while I still have my head."

Hank understood why Knowles had told him so much. He didn't expect anyone but him to get off the island alive.

Knowles vanished into the jungle, leaving Hank and Pedro feeling very alone again. They stood and listened for the sound of the Zi Xen. But the chanting had stopped.

Then Hank heard a different sound. Suddenly, Pedro looked up in a tree above them, and Hank saw his eyes get wide with fright.

CHAPTER 11

# *A Message From the Sky*

THERE in the light of the moon was a jaguar, looking down at them.Hank froze. He held his breath and hoped Pedro wouldn't say anything to startle the cat.

*That's strange,* Hank thought. *The jaguar is looking right at me, but it hasn't jumped.*

In another minute, the big cat yawned. After showing a mouthful of sharp teeth, it turned and leaped to another branch, and then it disappeared into the jungle.

"It must not be hungry," Hank said.

"Maybe it find rest of Scarface," Pedro suggested. "After headhunters finish with him."

Pedro pointed down to the campfire. "Look down there. Indians leaving," he said.

Hank looked down at the camp. The Zi Xen were leaving, taking Coatibamba and their other prisoners with them. They were going further up the riverbank to higher ground in the jungle.

Hank and Pedro decided to follow from a safe distance. After following the Zi Xen for over an hour in the dark, forbidding jungle, Hank and Pedro found themselves high on a mountain trail. The Indians were descending the huge mountain beyond them, leading Coatibamba and his men down into a deep valley.

Hank looked down into the valley, to a flat plain. In the moonlight, he saw strange markings on an opening in the valley.

"Look at those markings, Pedro," Hank said, pointing. "They're in the shape of a bird, a condor!"

Hank recognized the drawing on the valley floor by its dark sections representing the bird's plumage. The wings were darker, and the wing tips lighter. He remembered the day in Orinaca's office when the professor showed him the fake dagger. It seemed so long ago.

The condor on the valley floor fascinated Hank. Remembering something he had read once, he looked up into the dark sky. It was full of stars, but he immediately focused on a cluster of stars.

"What's up there?" Pedro asked, looking up.

"Look," Hank pointed, almost directly

overhead. "Do you see that group of bright stars? It's a constellation. I don't know its name, but it's shaped like a condor. It's just like the carving on the valley floor."

"*Si,* it look like giant bird, like the one on the ground," Pedro agreed.

"Come on," Pedro said. "Headhunters going down the mountain."

The boys followed them down the mountain. They saw that the Indians were approaching the ruins of an ancient city. Stone houses had crumbled and fallen. Only the shells of some of them remained standing.

In the center of the area was a tall pyramid, which was flat on top. Stone steps led up to the top, where there was a square stone building.

The Zi Xen were pushing Coatibamba toward the pyramid and raising their spears and machetes toward the high stone structure. Some Zi Xen in feathered headdresses carried lighted torches and wore beads around their necks, arms, and ankles. Others were dressed in jaguar skin and the feathers and skin of condors as they danced toward the pyramid. There were so many torches that Hank and Pedro could see clearly what was happening.

"The pyramid must be their place of

worship," Hank said. "The Zi Xen probably perform their sacrifices at the top, in front of that temple."

Suddenly, it became clear to the boys. The Zi Xen were going to sacrifice Coatibamba and his men to their Sun God.

"Quick, Pedro. Tell me everything you know about the Zi Xen," Hank said. "Whether it's supposed to be true or not."

"Uhh, let's see. They take people to top of temple and kill them with dagger. Then they throw them in big hole at top of pyramid. They fall all way down to bottom."

It made Hank shiver. He thought about what Pedro had said as he watched the Zi Xen tie Coatibamba to a stake at the base of the pyramid.

"I wonder why they're waiting to take Coatibamba to the top?" asked Hank.

Pedro didn't know. Hank gave it more thought. The Zi Xen sacrificed to their god by taking victims up to the top of their pyramid temple. They sacrificed them to the Sun God. Hank rolled all that over and over in his mind, trying to solve the mystery of how the Zi Xen perform the sacrifice.

Then an idea came to him. "They sacrifice to their Sun God!" he exclaimed. "Maybe they wait until the sun comes up!"

"Then Coatibamba not be killed yet," Pedro said, looking into the sky that was still full of stars. "Sun not rise for hour or more yet."

"Then we have time to try to rescue them!" Hank cried excitedly.

"How we do that? We have no gun, no knife." Pedro shook his head.

"We have a little time," Hank told him. "We have to think of a way. There's nobody else to save them."

The boys watched from their mountain hideout as the Zi Xen built a bonfire. *But they're starting a ceremony of some kind,* Hank thought. Below, at the pyramid, Coatibamba was tied to the stake near the base, and the other men sat by the fire with their hands tied behind them.

After a while, the boys saw some other Indians coming out of the ruins of a building near the temple. It only took Hank a moment to recognize who they had with them.

"It's Professor Orinaca!" Hank cried. "But he's not a prisoner! Knowles said they trust him, to find their dagger and return it to them."

The boys watched as Orinaca was offered a place at the bonfire.

"Look!" Pedro cried, seeing more Indians coming out of the ruins. "More prisoners!"

"Mom and Dad!" Hank exclaimed. "They're alive! They're here! I can't believe it! They're alive! They're alive!"

Pedro jumped up and down. "You pretty smart cookie! You say we find them here!"

Hank hugged his friend, tears welling up in his eyes. He looked back, to make sure that he hadn't been seeing things.

"It *is* them!" Hank declared. "And they look okay. They haven't been hurt."

Pedro looked up to the sky. Hank followed his gaze, and his heart sank.

"It'll be dawn soon," Hank said, seeing the sky grow a little lighter. The stars were becoming fainter.

Hank's heart sank again when he saw the Indians pound two more big stakes into the ground at the base of the temple. Several of the Zi Xen began pushing his parents toward the stakes, their hands tied behind them. Then they tied them to the stakes with vines.

Somehow, someway, he and Pedro had to rescue his parents, Coatibamba, and the others, all before the sun rose. And the dawn was breaking fast. Time was getting short.

"We need a weapon!" Hank cried as he and Pedro sat helplessly on the mountainside, looking down at the beginning of the terrible ceremony. "We have to save them."

"Maybe I go down and steal a spear," Pedro suggested. He got up and started to go down and try his luck.

Hank stopped him. "It would never work. There are a lot of them. We need a weapon," he repeated. "Or...or...something *better* than a weapon."

Pedro asked, "What could be better than a weapon?"

"The dagger!" Hank exclaimed. "The Dagger of Death!"

"Sure, but how we find it? Maybe your father find it. But he prisoner now," said Pedro hopelessly.

"It's here somewhere!" Hank said. "It has to be somewhere near the temple. Some Zi Xen must have buried it, hundreds or thousands of years ago, to keep it safe. Maybe some other tribe was after it, or something. The Zi Xen didn't want their dagger falling into the hands of their enemy. So, they buried it somewhere."

"Lots of places to bury it," Pedro said, looking down into the valley.

Hank felt his eyes drawn in the other direction. Not down into the valley, but up into the sky.

"That constellation," Hank said, studying the group of the stars that seemed to form a giant bird. "It's the shape of a condor with its wings stretched out. It reminds me of the condor that's carved on the handle of the Dagger of Death."

Pedro agreed, studying the constellation in the sky. Hank looked back down on the valley floor and studied the earth markings for a long time.

"The Zi Xen must have carved that figure of a condor on their valley floor, just beyond their sacred temple," he said, thinking out loud. "But why?"

"They like to draw?" Pedro suggested.

"There has to be a reason," said Hank. "There has to be."

Hank kept talking, hoping that one word or idea might lead to another, and help him solve the puzzle of the condor in the stars and the carving on the valley floor.

Suddenly, Pedro said, "If I go to big trouble to draw condor on the ground, I bury dagger inside the condor someplace."

"That's it! That's got to be right!" shouted Hank. He pounded Pedro on the back. "We don't have time for any more thinking. We have to look somewhere for the dagger."

It made sense to Hank. His parents were there at the temple. His father may have found the dagger and been captured. Or, maybe he was looking for it when the Zi Xen captured him. And maybe his mother had gone to Isla del Sol looking for him and had been captured, too.

"It's down there somewhere," Hank said with greater certainty. "The Zi Xen buried it somewhere inside the outline of the condor on the ground. But where?"

"Bad news, amigo," said Pedro. "The stars aren't so bright," he said, looking up again. "Soon, they fade away, and the sun come up."

Hank had been watching his parents, struggling as they were tied to the stakes beside Coatibamba at the base of the pyramid temple. Now he lifted his eyes again to the sky and saw that Pedro was right. A sense of helplessness swept over him as he saw the stars grow dimmer and the sky start to get brighter.

Then, as if the sky were sending him a signal, Hank saw something that made him cry out with excitement.

"Pedro! I see it now!" he yelled, leaping up and down with joy. "Now I understand! Now I know where the dagger is buried!"

## CHAPTER 12
# *Almost Dawn*

"PEDRO, look where I'm pointing!" Hank shouted. "See, up in the sky!"

Pedro looked up into the fading constellation in the shape of a condor.

"I no see nothing different. Just fading away, that's all," Pedro said. "It still doesn't tell me where dagger is."

"You still don't see it?" Hank asked anxiously. "The stars in the constellation of the condor. They were all bright an hour ago. But look now!"

"One of the stars is brighter than the others!" Pedro shouted.

"Exactly!" Hank cried. "When the other stars in the condor got dimmer, the one single star started to look brighter. And do you know what it means? It's telling us exactly where the Dagger of Death is buried!"

Pedro still looked confused.

"That brighter star explains it all," Hank continued. "It's where the heart of the condor would be, if it were alive and flying in the sky."

"In the heart, *si!*" Pedro agreed.

"Now, look down there," Hank said, "at the condor carved on the valley floor. I think the dagger is buried in the ground where the Zi Xen hid it from their enemies years ago," Hank said excitedly. "We'll find it in the place where the condor's heart would be."

"I hope you right, amigo," said Pedro, looking down at the valley floor.

"Well, it's only a hunch," Hank admitted. "But it's the only hunch we've got. So, let's get busy. We don't have much time!" Hank grabbed Pedro by the arm and started down the mountain in a desperate scramble that almost started an avalanche.

When Hank looked up again at the sky, the stars were disappearing fast, hidden in the approaching dawn. It made him more anxious than ever as he started down the mountain. Then, looking back at the Zi Xen temple, Hank saw something else.

"They're untying the prisoners!" Hank cried.

The boys stopped a moment and watched. Some Zi Xen had come out of the ruins in feathered headdresses, their bodies painted in bright colors. They were carrying long spears that were decorated with feathers. They approached the two white prisoners, and Hank watched helplessly as his father and mother were untied from their stakes. Then the Zi Xen untied Coatibamba from his stake. Guards pushed the three of them toward the base of the pyramid temple.

"It's almost dawn," Hank said. "They're about to start the sacrifice!"

Then they saw Orinaca get up from where he was sitting. He began walking to the base of the temple, toward Hank's parents.

"He's going to talk to them," Hank said. "Let's go closer and see if we can hear. Maybe we have more time than we think to look for the dagger. Or, maybe we don't have any time at all. We have to find out."

Pedro pointed to a small hidden area in the back of the pyramid. It looked like they could listen without being seen. Hank nodded. They ran through some brush until they reached the valley floor, and then made a dash for the back of the pyramid.

"It's a good thing the Zi Xen didn't post a guard back here," Hank said when he and Pedro were in the back of the pyramid.

The boys were still too far away from the

front where the prisoners were being held, so they crept around to one side. Now Hank heard Orinaca talking as he stood before Jeff Cooper.

"You don't have much time, Jeff," Orinaca warned him. "The sun will be up in just a few minutes. Then, your wife will die. Next, Coatibamba dies. And then each one of Coatibamba's men. You'll be the last to die. We'll wait until you tell where the dagger is!"

Now Hank knew the plan for the executions. His mother was to be taken to the top of the pyramid first.

*How can I save her?* Hank wondered.

"Don't tell him, Jeff," Hank's mother said to her husband. "It wouldn't do any good. They'd have the dagger, but they'd kill us, anyway."

Hank figured that was true, but he wondered what his father would do.

"Coatibamba say do not tell where dagger is," the guide said, with his hands still bound. "Once they get dagger, we all die."

Hank and Pedro listened while Hank's father tried to reason with the Zi Xen chiefs. He spoke in a language Hank couldn't understand. Pedro said he recognized it as a kind of Spanish that he had heard in the market. It was mixed with a lot of Indian words, but

Pedro was able to explain to Hank most of what they were saying.

"Do not trust this man," Hank's father told the chiefs in their own language, nodding his head toward Orinaca. "He says he tries to find your dagger for you, but he lies. He will take it from you, to sell it and become rich."

The professor laughed at Hank's dad and told him in English, so the Xi Zen wouldn't understand him, "You think the dagger means only money to me? You don't know me at all, Jeff. You don't understand anything about me. I'll sell the dagger, all right. And I'll make a fortune from it. But I'll get something even better. I'll be famous as the one who found the lost Dagger of Death. Then I'll be more famous than you, Jeff. My name will be the one everybody knows."

Orinaca laughed a devilish laugh that made Hank's blood run cold. Hank understood what Orinaca was after. He was jealous of Hank's father. That was why he seemed to hate Hank, why he didn't rescue him when he fell. Orinaca probably thought of the famous Dr. Jeff Cooper every time he looked at Hank. The terrible jealousy had driven Orinaca crazy.

"We're done for, anyway," Hank's mother was saying. "Don't give Orinaca the satisfaction of claiming he found the dagger."

Jeff Cooper tried reasoning with the chiefs. "Wait! I know where the dagger lies," he said to the chiefs, and Pedro interpreted for Hank. "It took me a long time to figure out where it is hidden. But one night I understood."

When Pedro translated this, Hank was more certain than ever that he had figured out the mystery of where the Dagger of Death was buried. One night in the jungle, his father had looked up into the star-filled sky and solved the mystery, just as Hank had done.

"I will give the dagger to you," Jeff Cooper told the chiefs, "because it belongs to you. It is sacred to you. It does not belong in a museum, but back with you. But I will give it back to you only if you promise to let us go. You must put Orinaca under guard, and free my wife and me and these other men."

Orinaca began to rage. Hank didn't need Pedro to tell him that Orinaca was insane with anger. "Do not do what he asks!" he cried to the chiefs. "He lies! He will not give up the dagger to you!"

One of the chiefs raised his hand to silence Orinaca. Then the chief looked at the eastern sky, where the sun would be coming up soon. The chief looked at Hank's father. Pedro translated.

"The sun soon rises," the chief said. "At first ray of sun, woman dies, unless you tell where dagger is. If still not tell, others die. Last, you die."

The chief then clapped his hands together. At this command, two guards holding Hank's mother began pushing her closer to the base of the pyramid.

Hank had heard and seen enough. Time was running out. He had to find the dagger before the sun came up, or all the prisoners would die.

After he saw the guards lead his mother up the first step of the pyramid, Hank led Pedro back behind the temple. Then they ran as fast as they could onto the plain on the valley floor, to where the condor was carved in the ground.

The carving was harder to see from the ground. From the mountain, it had looked like the outline of the condor. Below on the plain, Hank now saw only rows of lines that had been carved or dug into the earth maybe thousands of years ago. Weeds and grass covered some of the lines.

Hank ran to a place on the plain where he thought the heart of the condor would be. But the area was too large.

"It would take us days to dig all over around

here," he told Pedro.

"But we only have minutes," Pedro said, "not days."

The sound of chanting and drums floated across the valley floor in the gray dawn. Hank could imagine what was happening on the other side of the pyramid. The Zi Xen were pushing his mother higher up the temple. Her arms were tied behind her, and she could not escape.

He began digging in the hard ground with his fingers, with Pedro digging nearby.

"The morning light," Pedro said. "It is coming."

"Dig!" Hank cried. "Dig as fast as you can! It's got to be around here somewhere!"

The drums began to beat faster and louder as the boys dug. The beat of the drums made Hank and Pedro dig faster and faster.

"Where is it? Where is it?" Hank screamed through tears of desperation. His fingers were bleeding from digging in the hard dirt and rock.

CHAPTER 13

# *The Fourth of July*

HANK couldn't keep digging. He had to stop, even if only for a moment, to catch his breath and rest. As he and Pedro caught their breath, they saw a ray of sunlight strike the earth a short distance ahead of them.

The sun! Hank looked behind and saw that it was not on the horizon yet. Some clouds were blocking the first rays of sunlight. But they wouldn't block the sun forever, Hank realized. The drum beats grew faster.

Then Hank saw something strange about 10 feet from where they were sitting. A ray of sunlight struck the brown dirt. There was a flash of blood red light.

"The ruby! Pedro, the ruby!" Hank screamed hysterically. The boys began clawing the earth with their bloody fingers. Moments later, Hank's fingers closed around the object. He tore it from the ground and held it up triumphantly.

"The Dagger of Death!" Pedro shouted.

They heard the drums and chanting from the pyramid.

"Come on, Pedro!" Hank yelled. "Let's go!"

As the boys reached the base of the pyramid, they saw how the night clouds were starting to disappear slowly from the horizon. The edges of the clouds were bright from the sun starting to shine behind them.

Looking up and around the pyramid, Hank saw his mother. She was just reaching the top, climbing the stone steps with her hands still tied behind her. Two guards with spears were pushing her up.

Hank had never seen such a terrible sight. On some of the steps of the pyramid stood a Xi Zen warrior with his spear decorated with feathers and his skin painted in stripes and circles in many colors. On the other steps stood more Zi Xen, holding torches that burned brightly.

While they watched, a priest, clothed in condor feathers, came out of the square stone temple on the top of the pyramid. In his raised right arm he held a long, sharp knife. Hank thought he knew when the priest's arm would come down. His mother would die when the first ray of morning sunlight struck the blade of the priest's knife.

Halfway up the back side of the pyramid, Pedro said, "Hank, we not going to make it. No time to get to top before sun come up."

Hank stopped for a moment. He was out of breath. He couldn't tell if the sound he heard in his ears was the drumming of the Xi Zen or the beating of his heart.

"Even if we get up there in time, they won't hear us, anyway," Hank said. "That drumming is too loud. If only we had some way to make them hear us, so we could stop the ceremony."

"*Si,*" answered Pedro. "Need something real loud, so they stop. Wait! Hank! I know! In backpack, I bring firecrackers. Remember?

Hank let out a scream of happiness and opened Pedro's backpack. He took out the carefully wrapped bundle of fireworks and began to unwrap them.

"They're still dry!" Hank said. "Oh, no, Pedro! I hope you didn't forget to bring matches!" Hank cried.

"What good firecrackers without matches? No match, no boom!" answered Pedro, grinning. He took off the black hat he had gotten from one of the Indians and pulled out a pack of matches. "Hotel El Dorado matches," he said. "Very good matches."

"Then what are we waiting for?" Hank cried,

and he started dashing to the top of the pyramid as the drums grew louder still.

Just before the boys reached the top, they heard the drumming stop. The silence in the valley was incredible. The boys stopped a few steps below the top of the pyramid. They could see the priest and Hank's mother clearly. Several guards with spears also stood on the top.

"Look, Hank," Pedro whispered. "The sun!"

"You light. I'll toss," said Hank.

Moments later, the silence was broken by a tremendous cracking, banging explosion of firecrackers and cherry bombs. Sparklers and rockets split the gray dawn. Smoke, ash, and burning sulfur and gunpowder were everywhere.

Hank and Pedro were cheering and laughing wildly as they saw the guards take off running down the pyramid. They jumped up and down as the explosions continued.

"This is better than the Fourth of July, Pedro!" Hank shouted above the noise.

"What's Fourth of July?" asked his friend.

"I'll tell you later. Come on," said Hank.

They climbed to the top of the pyramid. Suddenly, appearing out of the thick smoke, Hank saw his mother. The priest had fallen to the ground and was covering his eyes.

"Hank!" she shouted. "I can't believe it!"

"Mom! Look what I've got! I've got it! I found the Dagger of Death!"

As the smoke cleared, Hank used the dagger to cut the vines that were tying his mother to the stake. Then he walked to the front edge of the pyramid and held the dagger over his head for all to see. As Hank stood on the edge, looking out over the fantastic scene below him, the first rays of sunlight broke through the morning sky and struck the dagger's blade.

CHAPTER 14
# The Mystery Solved

HANK saw that the Zi Xen guards were crouching about halfway down the pyramid, not daring to come any closer. They, and all the other Indians, were staring at their long lost sacred dagger. Looking down at his feet, Hank saw that the priest had dropped his knife. Hank kicked it over to Pedro, who motioned for the priest to stand up.

Hank, his mother, Pedro, and the priest all started slowly down the steps of the pyramid. The Zi Xen priest went first, with his hands in the air. Behind the priest walked Pedro, who was guarding the priest with the wicked-looking sacrificial knife. Hank's mom followed Pedro, and Hank brought up the rear, holding the dagger above his head so all could see.

As they got closer to the ground, they heard the Indians talking and muttering among themselves. Hank saw some Zi Xen guards push Orinaca and Hank's father to the front of the crowd. The chief stood with them. Hank smiled and waved to his father, who looked like he couldn't believe his eyes.

When they reached the bottom of the pyramid, the crowd opened to let them pass. All the Zi Xen were staring at Hank and the dagger. Pedro still kept the priest covered as they walked to where Orinaca, the chief, and Hank's father were standing.

"Pedro," said Hank, "tell them to let Dad go."

Pedro spoke to the chief, and then he said something to the priest, his prisoner. The priest looked frightened and raised his hands higher in the air.

"I tell him to stick 'em up," Pedro said to Hank, "just like John Wayne."

The chief gave an order to his men, and they untied Hank's father. His father rubbed his wrists.

Meanwhile, Orinaca was shouting, "Give me that dagger! It's mine. It should belong to me. I want that dagger."

Orinaca made a desperate lunge for the dagger. But two Zi Xen guards pushed him to the ground and tied his hands behind his back. Orinaca started whimpering quietly.

Hank threw his arms around his father.

Tears came to his eyes.

"Here, Dad," said Hank, "this is yours." He handed him the Dagger Of Death.

"No, Hank, it's theirs," he said nodding toward the Zi Xen chiefs. "We're going to give it back to them."

Hank's father walked up to the chief and spoke a few words. The chief looked Hank's father in the eye for a long time, and then he signaled for them all to follow him into one of the old ruins. Hank and his parents, Pedro, Coatibamba, and several Zi Xen who looked important followed the chief. The chief pointed his spear toward Orinaca and gave an order to one of the Indians. Orinaca was pushed toward the ruin with the others. Pedro let the priest walk away, but he held onto the knife.

"What's going to happen, Mom?" asked Hank.

"I don't know, Hank," said his mother. "It looks like your father will try to bargain with the chief. I'll try to translate for you."

They all sat down in a circle inside the ruin. Hank's father spoke first. Hank's mother translated.

"This is your dagger," said Hank's father to the chief. He held the dagger in his hand. "I found it, and I will give it back to you. But first, you must give me your word that you will not harm us and will let us go."

After what seemed like a long time, the chief nodded his head slowly. Hank's father continued in English, and his mother now translated for the Zi Xen.

"I was convinced that the dagger was not a fairy tale, and that its legend was based on fact," he said. "I made several expeditions to Bolivia to search for it. At the time, I trusted Professor Orinaca. We had worked together on other expeditions, and I thought we had become friends."

Hank saw that Orinaca hung his head.

"I never suspected that Orinaca had other plans for me and the dagger," Hank's father continued. "But I had a feeling, before I left on this last expedition, that if I found the dagger, maybe my life would be in danger. And I wasn't expecting danger from only the Zi Xen. I knew other people were after the dagger, too. So, I thought of a decoy."

"The copy!" Hank said.

"I didn't want to risk disappearing in the jungle without a chance of being rescued," Hank's father went on. "So, I decided to have a copy made. It was too dangerous an expedition to let you in on, Julie."

"I'm glad you didn't let me know what was

in the box," said Hank's mother. "I would have been too nervous to handle it, especially with Hank's safety to think about."

Hank's dad continued. "All I told Julie before I left on this last expedition was that if anything happened to me, she was to go to the air terminal in Bogota and get the box I had left there. I hoped the dagger inside would be a clue about why I had gone into the jungle and what I was searching for. Now I see I made a mistake in trusting Orinaca and telling him about the box and the dagger inside. It was a good thing I never told him the dagger was only a copy."

At that moment, there was a commotion outside the ruin where they were sitting. Hank heard Indian voices. All of a sudden, several Zi Xen burst into the ruin. One of them pushed a man on the ground in front of the chief.

"Knowles!" shouted Hank. The Englishman looked dirtier and more ragged than ever.

"White Suit more like Brown Suit now," whispered Pedro to Hank.

Orinaca gave Knowles an angry look and said, "You shut up. Don't you tell them a thing. I'll get you out of this if you keep quiet."

Knowles looked up at Orinaca. "You! What can you do to help me now? You're in the same mess I'm in." Then Knowles looked at Hank's father and started pleading, "Don't let them cut off my head. I'll tell you anything you want to know."

"Tell us everything," ordered Hank's father.

"He's the one!" Knowles exclaimed from the dirt, pointing at Orinaca. "He paid me and the others to steal the dagger. He told us to kill Hank and anyone who got in our way!"

"Shut up, Knowles," growled Orinaca.

Knowles told how Orinaca had hired him, Morrison, and Helga Schmidt to steal the box and how they failed. He told how Orinaca had tried to cheat them by not telling them the dagger was only a copy.

Orinaca interrupted Knowles. "Then you fools went into business for yourselves, to get the dagger, thinking it was the real one. That's what I get for working with amateurs."

"What happened to you at the airport in Bogota, Mom?" Hank asked.

"The German lady jumped me," she replied. "She gagged me and stuffed me into the mop closet."

"That's why I didn't see you when I went in to look for you," Hank said.

"I kicked until someone let me out," she explained. "By then, you had left on the plane for La Paz, and I was glad. I thought that we could trust Professor Orinaca. If I had known what he was really up to, I never would have told you to take the box to him."

"Then how did you get to the island, Mom?" asked Hank.

"Well, I wasn't completely in the dark about what Jeff was searching for," she said. "I found a book open on the desk at home. It was about the Dagger of Death and how it was missing somewhere on the Isla del Sol."

"So, after we got separated in Bogota, you started for here," Hank said.

"That's right. I'd been near here before," she said. "I hired some natives to take me by boat to the island. I had just landed when some Zi Xen captured me. They treated me well. I didn't get the impression that they were going to harm me until early this morning, after they reunited me with you, Jeff. That's when Orinaca tried to tell the chief to kill us because we wouldn't tell them where the dagger was hidden."

Hank saw that the Zi Xen chief was frowning and staring at Orinaca. The chief spoke with two of the other Zi Xen. Then he said something to Hank's father that seemed to disurb Hank's parents.

"What is it, Mom?" asked Hank. "What did the chief say?"

"The chief said that Orinaca and Knowles must die for their part in trying to steal the dagger," said Hank's mother.

"You would have had us killed," Hank's father was saying to the professor. "And you would have had Hank killed, too. I'm tempted to let the Zi Xen do what they want to you. You don't deserve any better, either of you. But I'll try to get the chief to let us take you back to the police."

Hank's father turned to the chief. Hank could tell he was pleading for the lives of the two men. Orinaca knew too, because he was starting to squirm.

"Jeff, help me. Help me," he pleaded. "Don't let them take me to the top of the pyramid."

Hank's father looked at his old friend who had turned against him. "You were willing to let me and my family go to the top of the Zi Xen's pyramid."

"Please! Please!" the professor cried.

"You're in luck, Orinaca," said Hank's father. "The Zi Xen are more civilized than you give them credit for. The chief is going to let me take you two back to the Bolivian police. I'm sure they'll put you away for a long time. Even if you do deserve anything the Zi Xen could do to you."

Orinaca and Knowles collapsed on the ground. The rest all stood up. Hank's parents shook hands with the Zi Xen chief, and they walked outside.

The Zi Xen had gathered in a large crowd around the ruin. Hank and Pedro watched as Hank's father and the chief walked to the base of the pyramid and climbed a few steps so all the Indians could see them.

Then, Hank's father handed the Dagger of Death to the chief. A look of great happiness came to the chief's face as he accepted the dagger. He held it up proudly. All the other Zi Xen began to cheer.

Hank knew how the Indians felt. A part of their tribe, their most important possession, had been missing for a thousand years. Now they had it back.

He and Pedro watched as the Indians began to file by the chief as he showed the dagger to each one.

"Hank, now you tell what this Fourth of July is?" asked Pedro.

Hank laughed at his friend. "It's our national... Oh, never mind, Pedro. It's not nearly as good as this!"

Coatibamba and his men were preparing to leave the pyramid area. Coatibamba checked to see that Orinaca and Knowles were securely tied, and then they were ready.

"We go now. Just have time to make it across Lake Titicaca before night. Zi Xen chief give us boats," said Coatibamba.

They began to climb the mountain path that would lead them out of the sacred ancient city of the Zi Xen. Right before they disappeared into the thick jungle, Hank turned around for a final look at the incredible sight. All the Zi Xen were on their knees facing the priest. The priest held the Dagger of Death high above his head. The ruby in the dagger's handle reflected a blood red flash of fire as it caught the sunlight.

At the first clearing, after they entered the jungle, the party stopped suddenly. Ahead of them was a horrible sight. Poles with racks held dozens of human skulls. Hank could guess what they were. They were the headhunters' victims from the past. He shivered to think that all of their skulls could have ended up on those poles.

They walked along in silence. After a while, Hank heard Coatibamba's voice behind him. He and Pedro turned around.

"Better behave. No trouble, or Coatibamba feed you to piranha!"

Then the giant guide smiled and laughed.

## About the Author

WALTER OLEKSY is a former reporter for the *Chicago Tribune* and a former editor of three travel magazines. He now writes books full-time. Among his books for adults are a cookbook, a true adventure story of a canoeing trip, and a history of the one-room schoolhouse. He has written a biography of Mikhail Gorbachev for young readers.

He enjoys camping, wilderness canoeing, gardening, and playing Frisbee with his dog Max. He lives in Evanston, Illinois.